DARK VENGEANCE

The slug that removed the right side of the dead man's face had proceeded through his brain and vaporized the display case where gold coins had once slept in velvet. The killer had, according to the ballistics report, used a silenced automatic, which would explain why nobody heard the shot and why Morgan Pajaro was unfortunate enough to discover the body all by herself, early the next morning, when she arrived to work at the gallery.

I had lied to the police, not to protect the perpetrator, but rather to save him for myself. The killer was someone I wanted. He had lied to me and used me, murdered a man based on information I had given him. And, last but not least, he had bedded my girl.

I had a thirst for his blood that just wouldn't quit.

DARK MONEY

ARTHUR ROSENFELD

AVON BOOKS ⬙ NEW YORK

DARK MONEY is an original publication of Avon Books. This work has never before appeared in book form. This work is a novel. Any similarity to actual persons or events is purely coincidental.

AVON BOOKS
A division of
The Hearst Corporation
1350 Avenue of the Americas
New York, New York 10019

Copyright © 1992 by Arthur Rosenfeld
Published by arrangement with the author
Library of Congress Catalog Card Number: 91-93028
ISBN: 0-380-76486-5

First Avon Books Printing: April 1992

AVON TRADEMARK REG. U.S. PAT. OFF. AND IN OTHER COUNTRIES, MARCA REGISTRADA, HECHO EN U.S.A.

Printed in the U.S.A.

RA   10 9 8 7 6 5 4 3 2 1

The Nestor Dark books
are dedicated to the memory of my uncle,
Arthur Matthew Master.
I miss you, Unk.

DARK MONEY

Chapter 1

I LOVE THE sweet heaviness of Connecticut in the summertime. I love the history, the farmhouses, the stone walls grown over by moss. I love the way the wise trees curtain my land. I love to sit in my house and sweat.

I was doing just that, and playing with a new piece of investment software, when Tolstoy pricked up his ears and growled. He may not be big, but Tolstoy is a Kerry blue terrier, and that means he has a mean bark, a meaner bite and ears that can hear you thinking a galaxy away. I looked up just in time to see a flash of red through the trees lining the long driveway up the hill. A few moments later, a red Porsche coupe came into view, slowly dodging the overgrowth and the potholes I leave there to discourage speedy arrivals and departures. I gave Tolstoy's thick head a pat. His eyes rolled back until they turned cream.

Sundays are like semicolons, freezing the action of my life just long enough for me to prepare for whatever's coming next. I guard Sundays jealously and I didn't want company.

I watched out the window of my second-floor office while the Porsche rolled to a crunching halt at the roundabout and a blond man of about thirty-five, wearing a blue blazer and gray slacks, got out.

"Ready!" I commanded Tolstoy. He looked up with a challenge in his eyes, but I stared him down and he trotted off. Then, dressed in baggy pants and a T-shirt in preparation for my morning workout, I went downstairs and opened the door.

The Porsche driver sized me up cautiously.

"Nestor Dark?" he inquired.

He was bigger than he had looked from the window: an easy two-fifteen. And he had bad skin.

"On Sundays I'm just Nestor."

"Name's Harry Hamilton." He stuck out his hand and I shook it briefly. "I have a proposition for you."

"Call my office on Monday. My assistant will give you an appointment."

He had an attitude, I could read it in his expression. Guys with bad skin can get that way from feeling bad about themselves when they're young. Later it can grow into other things. I've learned never to cross them.

"But I drove all the way from Manhattan to see you . . ."

"Suffering all the way in your Porsche."

"I'm afraid you don't understand." He frowned. "This is an urgent matter. We really must speak today."

"I'm afraid *you* don't understand, Mr. Hamilton. I won't do business today. I like to spend Sundays with my dog."

I closed the door gently in his face and waited for

the sound of his footsteps. Instead the mail slot creaked open and something too small to be a bomb dropped through to the floor. I picked it up.

It was a slab of plastic, encasing a tiny gold coin that sparkled and shone like newly unearthed treasure when I turned it in the morning light. One side depicted the head of a woman, the other a wreath cradling a large "1." The word *dollar* was etched at the bottom.

"An 1849 Type One dollar from the Charlotte Mint." Harry Hamilton's voice came through the door. "The mint didn't last very long, and that's one of the greatest numismatic rarities known. Any idea what it's worth?"

I fingered the piece.

"There are only four in existence," Hamilton continued through the mail slot. "The last one, and it was all beat up, sold at auction for a quarter of a million dollars. This one's worth much more."

I opened the door.

"Does it buy me a few minutes of your Sunday?" he asked smugly.

"My Sunday can't be bought. You're on borrowed time."

I let him in and gave him back his coin. He shoved it into his pocket and then tugged at his collar.

"No air-conditioning?" he asked.

"I don't believe in it."

I watched him look the place over. To my eye, the house gave a good accounting of itself: big rooms, polished hardwood floors, high ceilings, skylights, expensive hand-woven rugs and archaeological artifacts scattered about.

His fingers went to a kilim hanging on the white wall by the door.

"It's real," I told him. "You can tell by the space between the knots."

"You have good taste," he said.

"So do you."

He colored slightly and I began to feel sorry for the way I had treated him, so I asked him if he'd like a beer. He hesitated and checked the time.

"It'll cool you off. Go ahead and loosen your tie if you like."

"You're very highly respected in the investment community," he began.

"All that takes is money," I answered, and went to get a couple of Carlsbergs. When I came back, he was sitting on the couch.

"I'm not here for a handout."

I looked at his Rolex, his Southwick blazer, his Windsor knot. I considered his Porsche.

"If you are, you're wearing the wrong clothes."

"But I do want your help. You may have inherited a fortune, but you're still an ex-cop. I'm betting you will want in for the sport."

"I haven't been a cop in a long time."

"But you miss the street, don't you? The win-or-lose—right now—feeling? Admit you're just a little bored in your office all day long. . . ."

"Get to the point."

He looked at me over the beer. "What do you know about mutual funds?"

"Enough. I'm surprised it took you this long to mention you're on Wall Street."

"You in any funds?"

"That's none of your business. Please get to the point, Mr. Hamilton."

"I'm a fund manager, but my fund isn't based on

stocks and bonds. It's based on United States rare coins."

"I've read about this."

"Then you've read about me. It's a new idea on Wall Street, but since the grading services came along, coins are respectable now."

"Gives a sleazy business an air of legitimacy."

He winced. "Please. Unregulated, not sleazy."

"The press says different."

He shrugged. "They always do when something's new. Anyway, finally the customer is protected by a guarantee of quality and authenticity. Each coin is assigned a grade on a scale of zero to seventy. Dealers are linked by computers now, and they put up bids by teletype. Rare coins have become tradeable on a national scale, and as the saying goes, they ain't makin' any more."

"So you had the idea of setting up a fund based on the coins? Put people's money together, buy a portfolio, share the profits?"

"You got it."

"Don't tell me you're here to sell me coins, Mr. Hamilton."

At that point, Harry Hamilton made a mistake. He reached suddenly into the inside pocket of his Southwick summerweight.

He may weigh no more than fifty pounds, but Tolstoy isn't pretty when he's angry. He maims deer when he's angry and removes kneecaps just for fun. I had him recognizing a holster reach before he was nine weeks old. Teaching him to sit silently at the end of the couch and watch strangers took a bit longer.

He was on Hamilton in an instant.

"Jesus Christ!!" My guest howled as Tolstoy's

teeth went right through his jacket and into the tendons that controlled his fingers. The Charlotte dollar dropped to the floor.

I moved quickly to the couch and pinched Tolstoy's lips into his teeth from the top, releasing his grip on Hamilton's hand.

"I'm sorry," I said. "He thought you were going for a gun. Sometimes people do that to me."

Tolstoy looked angrily up at me, all fifty pounds of him vibrating like a slammed door.

Chapter 2

"I COULD SUE you," Hamilton gasped, nursing his forearm. There were some blood spots seeping through. I retrieved the coin from the carpet and put it down on the coffee table.

"Not the best way to get my help. Anyway, the dog's not rabid."

I went to the bathroom for some antiseptic. Hamilton winced as he took off his coat and rolled up his stained shirtsleeve. Tolstoy sat glaring at him from the floor.

"At least call him off!"

I booted the dog away and handed Hamilton an iodine-soaked swab. Strangely, the sight of his own blood seemed to mollify him, and even though one tooth had gone too deep for the wound to be considered trivial, he stayed winter-quiet and carefully tended his flesh. When he was done, he gestured at the coin.

"That piece is out of the fund portfolio."

"You buy things that rare for a fund? I would think a big-ticket item like that would go to a coin freak."

"Ordinarily it would, but the rarest coins appreciate the fastest, like Rembrandts and Picassos. Unfortunately that coin is beyond rare. It's a fake. A dud. Counterfeit."

"A counterfeit? But didn't experts put it in that plastic?"

Hamilton flashed me his first smile. "Experts can be wrong. I should know—I am one."

"And the guy who sold it to you can't make good?"

"You're still not reading me, Mr. Dark. This is big. Really big. Wall Street is conservative. If it got out that I was basing a twenty million portfolio on counterfeit coins, everything would be over. The idea, the fund, and me."

I thought for a moment. "All right. It's a fake. Why not just let it be? The coin's already graded. Nobody will know."

"The coin was one of a large lot I bought at auction. The idea is to trade the coins around with market cycles. Something looks cheap to me—Buffalo nickels, for instance—I buy them. Standing Liberty quarters go up, I sell them. Now let's say someone gets hold of one of the coins that I sell and decides to have it regraded. . . ."

"You can do that? Break it out of the plastic and send it in to the same company again?"

He nodded vigorously. "Happens all the time. Grade the coin one point higher, and the value can rise ten times."

"So somebody wanting to make a quick buck could end up tracing a fake back to you."

"And I'm either a sucker or a crook and the whole thing blows up in my face. It's not worth the risk."

"You *do* have a problem," I said.

He checked under his shirt and flexed his forearm muscles to see if blood would ooze. Satisfied that the bleeding had stopped, he rolled down his sleeve.

"I'm supposed to go to a wedding after this," he muttered.

"Look, Mr. Hamilton, I've given you a piece of my Sunday, a beer and a hole in your arm, and I still don't know what you're doing here."

He reached for the beer and took a long swig.

"This is a very sensitive problem. It requires a delicate touch, specialized knowledge and somebody who can keep their mouth shut. I think that somebody is you."

"I don't have specialized knowledge, and I've never thought of myself as having a delicate touch."

He smiled. "You're perfect, Mr. Dark. You understand Wall Street, money, economics and people. Plus you're a trained investigator with an airtight cover."

Sensing my anguish, Tolstoy appeared from nowhere and pressed his muzzle reassuringly against my hip.

"I'm a philanthropist," I said at last. "I don't see how I can help you."

"You can find the counterfeiter, Mr. Dark!"

"Find the counterfeiter!"

He smiled and took another long swig.

"Oh, come on, don't act so surprised! It's the obvious answer! Look, you catch the guy, I'm a hero. They'll write articles about how sharp I am. Christ, I'll be a coin saint. Imagine my credibility! It'll make the *Wall Street Journal*. The fund will soar!"

"I'm sure."

"The coin business is too small for me to talk to the police or hire a private investigator. I'm under the microscope on Wall Street, Mr. Dark. One wrong question and down comes the boom. But you! Nobody would ever link us, and with your money and reputation, they'll be falling all over themselves for your business. They'll tell you anything."

"You've gotten me confused with someone else," I said. "I don't catch counterfeiters. I give money away. I have a desk job. I have a chauffeur. I don't work the street and I'm not for hire. Maybe you didn't do your homework, Hamilton, or maybe somebody steered you wrong."

He held up his fist and popped up a finger.

"Orphaned at sixteen when your parents were killed in a car accident, you were raised by your father's brother, the financier Andrew Dark. He set you up in your own place and paid for you to learn and travel and do just about whatever you wanted. He didn't even quibble when you signed on at John Jay to study Criminal Justice."

"Hey!" I said.

He raised another finger. He was talking rapidly now, a tiny bit of beer foam on his lip. "You were a good cop, hard and smart, if a little spoiled, and you had a hell of a sharpshooter's eye. You made the SWAT team and a bump in pay, and you learned how to size people up and make split-second decisions under stress."

"My split-second decision is to ask you to leave," I said, rising to my feet.

Hamilton stayed calmly where he was and raised another finger. "After five years on the force you were a respected guy, a little arrogant, a little distant, but respected. Then your uncle came down with bone-melting cancer, the kind that just eats a guy up in a matter of months. You took care of him day and night—after all, he was all you had—and when he died he left it all to you. Two hundred and sixty million dollars. You took the money and established the Dark Foundation, determined to do better with the money than he had."

"He did just fine," I said.

"And if he didn't, your efforts would absolve him. But what happened to your life, Mr. Dark? What happened to living in the real world? The down and dirty. Five years ago you were a cop! You picked the life. Has the money bleached you so pale you've got no game left in you? This is a chance to catch a criminal no one else can catch, a secret criminal nobody even knows is out there!"

Tolstoy whined while Hamilton held me in those glowing Wall Street eyes.

"Quite a speech," I said.

"I practiced. Look, if you need to justify this, then call it investigating a new investment vehicle for your foundation. I'll put a portfolio together for you. Do you better than thirty percent a year."

"How do you know the forger's still alive? Maybe you've got a hundred-year-old fake."

"Common sense!" he cried, encouraged. "The coins weren't rare back then."

Tolstoy panted. Through the open windows I could hear a distant summer wind rustling my trees.

"Somebody tells me thirty percent, I hold them to thirty percent," I said.

"*And* I'll make a six-figure donation to the charity of your choice." Hamilton clapped his hands.

"I'll need the coin," I announced suddenly. "Call it a goodwill gesture."

I extended my palm and he handed it over without hesitation, the slightly sordid gleam of victory in his eyes.

Chapter 3

Hamilton left and I went out to the five-car garage. I don't have five cars in Connecticut, so I use the extra space for a gym. I've set up a heavy bag out there, chained to the beam. There's a mirror on one side, plus a speed-bag, a ballet barre, stretching contraptions and a weapons closet.

There's also a wooden dummy from mainland China: a five-foot-high red oak "trunk" with two "legs" and two "arms" sticking out at odd angles. The dummy provides the perfect partner for the practice of the martial art of Wing Chun. It's tough as hardwood, won't scream and can't be bruised. I should know; I've been wailing on it almost continuously since that day, in my sixteenth year, when my childhood ended.

Working the dummy is like moving meditation to me, and as I began the hundred-and-eight move sequence I envisioned myself bringing Hamilton's counterfeiter to justice. My energy seemed to seep into the wood, and it glistened with my sweat and

quivered with my blows. I stepped up the pace a little, but still felt nothing in my forearms. The nerves
there have long been dead.

Was I really so stuck that Hamilton could smell it
way out there on the country road in his Porsche, or
had he simply used what he knew of me to shrewdly
guess that I might be a little bored? Was my frustration with the endless meetings and responsibilities
obvious to everyone? Was the weight of Dark money
pressing me flat, or was there something else that I
alone felt, deep inside? The slips and locks of the
dummy weren't enough. I needed a stitch in my side
and a pounding in my heart. I slipped on a pair of
thin gloves and moved over to the heavy bag.

At first I just stood there, knees bent, executing
straight little punches with a vertical hand. Once I
had the rhythm going, I practiced pulling away, cut-
ting the moment of contact between my fist and the
bag down to nanoseconds—while still maximizing
the penetration, putting all one hundred and seventy-
five pounds of me into it. I was working on the kind
of speed that stops hearts and ruptures spleens. I was
working on the master's punch.

Someday I hope to be able to send that bag hop-
ping without actually touching it at all, but until then
I'll have to be satisfied with a rousing good sweat.

Exhausted, I moved to the barre and pressed my
stomach right up against it. I locked both knees,
raised my right leg and put the heel on the wood, toes
up. I bent sideways, slid my leg down and felt the
pull in my groin and hamstrings. I bounced slightly,
not enough to rip any muscle fibers, but enough to
warm up a little. When I had stretched the other leg,
I was ready to work out with the staff.

The weapon of choice among monks who disdained an edged blade, the staff can be a formidable piece in the right hands. I favor it for the feel of the wood and the way it strengthens and tones my shoulders and back. The best staffs are made of hickory, strong enough to break bone and flexible enough to persuade without shattering. I moved around the garage with the stick, picking targets at random. There was a bumblebee on the inside of the garage window, buzzing frantically and trying to escape. The challenge was to hit him with the end of the staff, but not to follow through and break the window. With or without six feet of wood between us, the only way to ace that bee was with the same quick in-and-out I strove for on the bag.

I took several deep breaths and tried to stop thinking of Harry Hamilton and his Charlotte gold piece. I relaxed, and the bright and smiling image of Uncle Andrew came briefly to mind. As it faded, I jabbed, and the bee fell dead, leaving a tiny smear of bee gut on the window.

My spirits fell when the hunt was over.

Chapter 4

MONDAY MORNING I dressed in a seersucker suit and a bow tie while Tolstoy inhaled his morning beef. The day was so spectacularly cloudless—and the decision to help Harry Hamilton so invigorating—that I bowed to the wild boy in my soul and decided to ride my motorcycle to work. New York City is a piss-poor place to be on two wheels, but I felt ready for anything.

I have several bikes, but only the BMW Paris-Dakar has the suspension to soak up the yawning crevasses that pass for pavement in the Big Apple. I strapped my briefcase to the backseat, bumped the bike off the centerstand, pushed it out of the garage and gave it full choke. Two-cylinder BMWs are primitive beasts, taking just as long to warm up today as they did when Rommel's Afrika Korps used them in the desert fifty years ago. While the engine sputtered and smoked, I donned my leathers and helmet, checked on Tolstoy one last time, then straddled the high saddle and took off.

Riding can be moving meditation on the order of the wooden dummy, and the roads around Redding were empty that morning, allowing me to concentrate on the Zen aspects of tilting the horizon with handlebars. The early commuters had already passed through, and the late ones wouldn't be out for another hour. I guided the BMW through twists and turns, soothed by the rumble of the engine and relaxed by the smell of freshly cut grass.

The Merritt Parkway was jammed, and I split lanes for miles, keeping my eyes focused at least a quarter of a mile ahead, looking for the slightest motion of head or bumper that might signal a car about to change lanes and make me motormeat. I moved faster than the flow of traffic all the way through Connecticut, into New York's Westchester County, and then down to the Bronx River Parkway, over the Willis Avenue Bridge and onto the island of Manhattan.

Five years ago, I put a lot of time and effort into the Dark Foundation offices. My real estate agent warned me against appearing raw. He told me that old money gravitates to old buildings, and suggested a building with elevators that looked like giant bird cages and marble staircases and shimmering chandeliers. I went along with him until I saw the tiny windows. Despite my name, I need lots of light, and I explained to him that I didn't want people visiting the Dark Foundation and thinking it was some kind of voodoo outfit.

So I chose the penthouse suite of a modern Fifth Avenue building with a private elevator that goes straight up to my personal office from the lobby or the garage. The entire office complex has airy rooms, picture windows and is decorated with fine art and fine furniture, all part of the foundation's investment portfolio and all protected by the most advanced security system money can buy.

When I carried my motorcycle helmet through the door, Isabelle was waiting with a pair of loafers in hand. She handed them to me.

"How did you know I'd ride?" I asked.

"You're late," she answered. "The way you drive, traffic wouldn't stop you. Knowing how you feel about Sundays and me, I figured it wasn't a woman making you late. That means you had a late start. A late start means you had trouble making up your mind about something, and you only have trouble making up your mind when something new comes up. Since you didn't take on any new work last week, someone must have come to see you at home. If someone came to see you at home, especially over a weekend, you probably tried to throw them out. If you let them stay, it must have meant you were interested."

I kept silent when she took the helmet from my hands and the leather jacket from my back.

"If you were interested, you probably needed to think. And when you need to think," she finished with a flourish, "you ride your bike!"

When I started the Dark Foundation, I was still naïve enough to put an ad in the paper for a secretary. The ad required not-for-profit administrative experience. The interviewing stole two of the dreariest weeks of my life, during which I met old women who called me "dearie" and young men who called me "sir." I saw young women who offered *me* hiring bonuses, and I saw old men who thought that all they needed was an empty suit to look respectable.

And then I met Isabelle Redfield.

It was a frigid winter day, and she came in wearing

sunglasses, woolen tights, purple leg warmers, a ski jacket, a cap and mittens. She had a big leather satchel over her shoulder. She asked me for a ladies' room and I pointed her down the hall. When she came back, I didn't recognize her.

The first thing I noticed was her hair. It was a deep, lustrous blond. Not the blond of travel or fashion posters, but a darker, more natural tone. Her skin was perfect, her cheekbones high, her lips full, her eyes the lightest green. She had changed into a very conservative charcoal business suit, but it couldn't hide the fact that her body was dream stuff. I know I stared.

"Function before form," she explained, even though her form looked fine to me. She opened the leather satchel just long enough for me to catch a glimpse of her ski clothing. "And I'd like to tell you a thing or two before you start asking me questions."

I don't remember asking her to sit down, but she did anyway.

"You don't want someone with not-for-profit experience," she began. "People who work for charities have no idea how to conduct business; they have no idea how to manage efficiently, how to save money, how to get results. You advertised for a secretary. I'm here to be your office manager."

I remember that by the time she had finished setting me straight, I was ready to marry her, and have been more or less ever since. I hired her at twice the salary I'd intended and gave her ten times the responsibility. And I've never been sorry, even when I found out that all she had done before was model her hands.

"Charlie Bender called," she told me, following me into my office.

"Any message?"

"He wants to meet you for lunch. One o'clock at the usual place."

I sat down behind my vast desk. The size isn't a power thing with me, just a matter of practicality. I like to spread things out.

"Any other calls?"

"The Nature Conservancy wants your decision on the Utah land."

"They'll get the land when I get the rattlers. What else?"

"Christie's wants to know if you'll make the party after the auction Thursday night."

I pursed my lips and Isabelle sat down.

"Early American furniture. You were thinking of some more for the Santa Barbara house, remember?"

"Give them my regrets."

"I already did."

"You're a mind reader."

"Remember that," she told me. "It keeps your thoughts pure."

"Purely of you. What else?"

"A Mr. Hamilton called, said he'd like to meet with you next week and asked that you pick the place."

"He leave a number?"

Isabelle shook her beautiful mane. "I tried my best. He said he'd call Friday."

"All right. If I'm not here when he calls, you pick the restaurant. Pick something Italian in Soho. And do me another favor. Block off my calendar for a few hours tomorrow afternoon."

"Going to the dojo?"

"Will you get out of my head?"

Finally I got a smile out of her. That's something I like to do a lot. I'm a woman pleaser at heart.

"Anything else?"

"Would you find out whether there's some kind of association of coin collectors, coin dealers, whatever?"

"Coin collectors," she repeated.

"I don't even know where to tell you to start looking—"

"The museum," she interrupted, making a note on her pad.

"Or a coin shop. I want reading matter: brochures, booklets, whatever. I want to know *everything* about the industry. Send a messenger for the stuff. Also, have them recommend some books on coins for the investor, American only. I'll need those, too."

She gave her best stern look. "Do you really think you need a new hobby and more toys, Nestor?"

"Get me the Nature Conservancy on the phone," I said brusquely, letting her know that I won't be treated as a child, especially by the woman I love.

She left the room with a hip wag that paid me back in spades.

Chapter 5

THE REST OF the morning involved calls to a real estate agent, a United States Park Ranger, a reptile population biologist, accountants and the Nature Conservancy, all regarding the transfer of the Utah land. The parcel represented a portion of the Dark Ranch, arguably Uncle Andrew's favorite home.

Last fall the Nature Conservancy offered to buy it for a paltry sum, promising to keep it wild forever. My uncle's dying dictum to do something worthwhile with his assets plagued me, and despite the fact that I loved the ranch every bit as much as he had, I agreed to sell, guessing that he would have approved of the sacrifice on principle.

But the sale had a condition. An extremely endangered species of rattlesnake was indigenous to the area, and I stipulated that a number of the beautiful reptiles be transplanted from nearby Arches National Park and protected forever. I wanted to do my part to protect animals nobody cared about.

By twelve-thirty I had gotten the Nature Conservancy to agree to pay for the capture of several hundred snakes, and been assured by the population biologist that the land could sustain them. Then, over the real estate agent's objection, I had the United States Park Service mark the land as a wildlife hazardous-disease area. Satisfied, I went to meet Charlie Bender for lunch at the Brasserie on Fifty-third Street.

Bender runs the Artificial Intelligence Laboratory for Columbia University, striving all day long every day to develop an electronic mind that works even half as well as his does. In that pursuit he's as stubborn as a Zen master, and just as courageous. A childhood polio victim, he's confined to a wheelchair by rubber legs.

Bender says he likes the Brasserie because it's mainstream and he isn't. I think it has more to do with the relationship that he's developed with the maître d'. He always gets the same table, and two waiters lift him into the seat facing the door. If someone is occupying the table when Charlie arrives, they are politely asked to move. If they won't, they are asked to leave.

Bender was in his favorite chair when I arrived.

"How." He held up his hand like an Indian.

"Something wrong? You called for lunch."

Bender sighed. "So that's what it's come to. The zillionaire gets all wound up in his money and gets too busy for his friends. It's to the point where a man like me has to have a reason for calling. I was downtown for a conference, that's all. Thought it'd be nice to take a break."

"And relax your mind in the presence of a mental midget," I said, sitting down across from him. Nobody offered us menus. They knew we didn't need them.

"Ah, the great and self-effacing Nestor Dark. You can't fool me with the mental-midget routine. I know how arrogant you really are."

"Well, then, tell me about the conference."

"Robotics," said Bender. "My colleagues on the mechanical side have made great progress in putting together able creatures that can run, swim, jump, even fly. They're waiting for me to supply a brain."

"Fly?" I asked.

A waiter brought us two bowls of onion soup overflowing with melted cheese.

"What do you think a cruise missile is?" said Bender. "A suicidal robot. I wish I could tell you more, but I can't."

"Well, then, tell me everything you know about rare coins."

Bender looked up in surprise.

"Not another hobby, Nestor. Please. I never thought of you as the coin type. Women, yes, even though you should wake up and marry Isabelle before she slips away. Fast cars and fast bikes, definitely. Punching and kicking people? Without a doubt. But coins?"

"United States rare coins," I said. "I'm on a case."

"You're what?" he asked mildly.

"I'm on a case, helping a guy out, catching a crook."

Bender took a long measure of his onion soup.

"You're catching a crook?"

I picked at some of the cheese that had hardened on the side of my bowl.

"You think there's something wrong with that? A guy came to me with a problem he thinks only I can solve. I'm just helping him out."

"I thought you got over the policeman disease," he

said, holding my eye for a moment before tilting his head back so a long string of cheese would go down.

"I just thought it would break up my day, you know, scout around on a case a little between meetings."

Bender took a swallow of beer.

"You've got responsibilities now. You're an administrator."

"I know what I am. I just thought I'd help this guy out."

"With coins?"

"Yes."

"But we got into this conversation because you don't know anything about coins."

"I have other skills he wants. Now will you tell me about coins?"

"I'd be careful, Nestor. Anyway, coins are popular these days. They're even basing mutual funds on them. You might invest a little foundation money in them just for diversification purposes, so long as you buy only so-called 'certified' coins in tamperproof plastic cases. Plastic seems to have taken the bullshit out of selling coins. It keeps dealers honest."

"You don't really sound like you approve."

"Tangible assets always do well in a down market. The worse the economy gets, the more people gravitate toward an investment vehicle they can understand. Macroeconomically, it's a trap, of course, because it diverts money from industry, which is the place that we need it most in order to make ourselves more competitive in the world marketplace, but rare objets d'art as investment vehicles are a coming thing. You'll see the same thing with paintings and sculptures. Even with your Japanese porcelain."

"How the hell do you know so much about this?"

"While you're out riding and shooting and flying, I'm book learning."

"Book learning," I snorted.

The waiter came and took away our soup.

"So did you tell these robotics people anything?"

"Well, the Department of Defense pays some of my bills," said Bender. "So I had to be honest. I told them that by the year two thousand, I might be able to provide them with a logic system that can think better than they can."

"Fantastic," I said.

"Of course, that won't be hard to do," he continued. "They're soldiers."

Salad and Carlsberg came just about then.

Chapter 6

AMOS LARSEN MAY be a priest, but his gym is no temple. It's a street-fighting school, pure and simple, and when I worked the precinct it was all I could do to keep Amos's students in line and stop my captain from shutting the place down.

Amos spent the first thirty-five years of his life chasing martial arts masters. Like the supplicants of ancient China, he did anything and everything to be noticed and, finally, to be taught. The sages he pursued—tiny wizened Chinese men who looked like crickets and moved like typhoons—didn't take kindly to huge white boys. He's never told me the details, but it's clear he groveled plenty in order to learn Preying Mantis Kung Fu, the twelve Shaolin animal forms, the internal systems of Pa' Kua and Hsing' I, Wing Chun, Tai Chi and the healing arts of Chi' Kung. Now he's capable of breaking bones with his fingers, with his eyes closed, while fast asleep in a locked closet across town. His street-thug students call him *sifu*—the Chinese word for "teacher"—and so do I.

Amos was waiting for me when I walked in Tuesday afternoon. He was dressed in his customary blue Chinese jacket with white rope buttons and baggy pants. That's all he ever wears, even when we go out.

"Sifu." I bowed to him.

"Sifu." He bowed back.

"I'm sorry I'm late."

"A thousand push-ups. Beee-gin!"

I smiled and tossed my gear bag to the floor, and Amos stood there, arms akimbo, while I shadow-boxed to warm up. Amos's arms are wondrous things, all the more so because they have the capacity to completely cover his fifty-six-inch chest, a torso borne purely of the traditional dynamic tension exercises of the Shaolin monk. Amos never touches weights.

I told him I was ready.

"I have a new breaking technique to show you," he responded. "I'm going to tape it for the kids."

He signaled to a couple of students trading kicks in a corner, and they hurried over with a video camera and a brick. I watched as they put the brick down on the windowsill, prepared the camera and set up flood-lights.

Amos walked over to the sill and took a measure of the brick. He hefted it in his hands, applied pressure with his thumbs to test its thickness, grunted with satisfaction and handed it to me. It was as heavy as I'd expected it to be. I'd seen Amos break things before.

The two students watched, transfixed, as Amos stroked his long blond braid, and massaged his thickly corded neck. He placed himself in front of the window and went down into a deep horse stance, his legs spread wide, his knees bent so that his giant chest was level with the sill. He tilted his head back and then slowly lowered it forward.

"You promised me you wouldn't do that anymore," I said.

Amos still bore a faint white scar from the last time he had broken a brick with his head. The brick had shattered, all right, but so had the thin skin covering his forehead. He'd required eleven stitches, and I'd had to take him to the hospital in my patrol car and explain everything to the doctor.

"Go for it, Sifu," whispered the student behind the camera.

Amos moved like a giant bird, slowly ducking his head and then bringing it up, ducking it and bringing it up, stopping just shy of the brick each time; practicing the motion and measuring the distance. I could hear him breathing deeply and evenly, filling and exhausting his reservoirs, flushing his system and purifying the air. I tried, but I couldn't get a look at his expression.

"Camera," he said, and just as the student clicked it on, Amos whipped his massive bald forehead down onto the concrete.

The brick shattered with a gunshot crack. Shards of stone went everywhere. A piece stung me on the shin. The students jumped backward and I caught the video camera as it toppled.

Amos's frame relaxed and he straightened. I went to him and inspected his forehead, but couldn't find anything.

"Not a mark," I announced.

"Of course not." He winked. "I never touched the brick."

"What?"

"No contact. It was a chi exercise. Let's watch," said Amos.

A student rewound the tape and connected the camera to the TV in the corner. We gathered in front of the monitor to watch Amos Larsen focus his chi into a brick. The tape was impressive, but it seemed to reveal contact, and I said so.

"Slow motion," Amos commanded.

We watched it again. This time the contact was unclear.

Martial artists have long contended that a mysterious force known simply as chi courses through our bodies along paths called meridians. It is these "channels" of energy that the acupuncturist manipulates to heal his patient, and the same channels which the Oriental fighter can utilize to deadly effect.

"Freeze the frame," I suggested.

Amos looked at me, then nodded, and the student complied.

We looked closely. The TV picture showed a tiny gap between Amos and the brick. The students were silent. My palms were sweating. I'd lost my taste for working out with Amos, but I wasn't going to get off so easy.

"Ready?" he asked me, clapping his hands.

We faced each other and entwined arms for "sticking hands," a prelude to Chinese boxing and an integral part of the Wing Chun Kung Fu system. "Battle of the Titans," I heard one of them whisper.

"I've got something going on," I told him as we

began to push each other back and forth. The students lined up to watch us.

"I could tell. You're excited, buzzing, like when you were on the street."

"I'm going to do something. Hunt someone down."

"Anything I can do?"

"Not now."

"But you'll let me know?"

"Of course."

Each of us held one arm high and the other low, leaving an open space between our hands about the size of a soccer ball. The exercise entailed switching this position rapidly back and forth. We pursued this rhythmic exchange for a time, speeding it up, pulling and pushing each other around the gym.

"Very light," said Amos. "Very nice." I was gasping for air, but he barely seemed to break a sweat. His arms were perfectly controlled, soft and yielding when he moved, but instant tree trunks if I tried to push him.

My mind wandered for an instant, and Amos pulled me off balance and then struck me hard in the belly with his open palm. Losing concentration when fighting a guy who breaks bricks without touching them is a poor idea. It was like getting hit in the stomach with a house.

"Isabelle and I are getting married," I said.

My eyes were on his when I said it, and his glance showed his surprise. He'd never admit it, but Amos is as weak-kneed around Isabelle as the next guy. In that moment I hooked my wrist around his arm and yanked him to me hard.

"Son of a bitch," he grunted as he pitched forward into a roll and came back up ready.

"Only kidding." I smiled, then ran for my towel and my bag.

I know enough to quit when I'm ahead.

Chapter 7

ISABELLE WOKE ME the next morning to tell me that the newspaper listed a coin show in a nearby New York town. It was drizzling, so I skipped the motorcycle and fired up my Ford Taurus SHO.

Bender ridicules it as too black and generic, but I like the Ford because it's not what it appears to be. I have removed the nameplate and the ground effects that identify it as the Special High Output factory hot rod, and souped it up even further. The twenty-four-valve Yamaha engine has been blueprinted to produce three hundred and twenty-five horsepower, and the suspension has been stiffened and upgraded to match. It goes like a running back after a high school cheerleader.

I guided the SHO down my long, rutted driveway and out onto the twisting Redding roads. The slick highway made for interesting driving, and I skidded through the familiar corners with glee and abandon, all the while listening to Bach's Fifth Brandenburg Concerto. Maybe I hadn't completely committed myself to Harry Hamilton's dirty work yet, but flirting with the idea of action was intoxicating.

I'm not sure exactly what I expected from the coin show, but it wasn't what I got. The exhibition hall was big enough to quarter an artillery division, with a ceiling big enough for an Apollo booster, or a basketball game among Gullivers.

And the lighting was strange. There were red carpets hanging from the walls, and flags, and gold banners, giving the giant room a mosaic effect by bending and twisting the fluorescent light from above and the yellow light from small table lamps below. I bought a ticket at the door and handed it to a security officer.

I could understand the need for tight security here. I didn't know enough about coins to accurately guess the value of the room, but certainly it was in the millions. Things can happen around that much money, and I was glad to have my stainless-steel Walther PPK in a clip holster tucked into the small of my back.

My plan was to mingle and get a feel for the way coins were bought and sold. In my mind's eye, coin collectors were either gangly adolescents who couldn't get a date, or little old men with thick glasses and hoarding ways. The people I saw milling about the coin tables surprised me. They ran the gamut from prosperous-looking yuppie investors in expensive leisure clothes to studious collector types with magnifying glasses and sacks full of reference books. Whatever their appearance, however, there was a common thread of almost-nerdiness that linked them, a nose-to-the-ground attention to detail that I had seen in Tolstoy and Harry Hamilton both.

I approached a table where a transaction was in

progress. The seller was a man with years of burgers, chips and beer rolling defiantly over his belt. He wore a plaid shirt and a bolo tie. His paper name tag identified him as Al of Shady Tree Coins.

The buyer was a nervous man in his forties with a briefcase, a mustache and a wad of cash. He held a coin in a plastic slab just like the one that had held Harry Hamilton's gold piece, and then looked at Al.

"I'll give you twenty-six fifty," he said at last.

I moved in closer. Al took the coin and flipped it between his fingers, then looked up and saw me.

"Be right with you," he said with a smile.

The buyer looked me rudely in the eye and made a lobster motion with his fingers. "Move along," he said.

"I'll give you twenty-seven hundred," I told Al.

He looked pleased. The buyer looked at me with blood in his eyes.

"Twenty-seven fifty," he said.

"Twenty-eight hundred," I said.

"Twenty-eight fifty," he responded.

"Twenty-nine."

"Three thousand," the buyer said with furious finality.

"He can have it for three thousand," I said and moved off. I heard some slamming and cursing, and then the buyer was gone. I returned to the table.

"Got any early gold?" I asked.

Al looked up.

"Jesus," he said. "You again. Man, you almost got me killed. That dude'd shoot you over an extra three fifty."

"He looked like a real tough guy," I said.

"Sometimes you get 'em like that." He wiped his brow with a handkerchief. "What can I do you for?"

"I'm looking for tough date Type One dollars."

Al sized me up. "At a show like this?"

"Uncirculated only," I said.

He laughed. "Nothing like that. Commemoratives, mercury dimes, a couple of nice three-cent nickels."

I shook my head.

"Guy under the lion flag's the only one here who's got any early gold," Al informed me.

I wandered over and found another class of operation entirely. Two security guards loitered just far enough from the table not to interfere with business. The dealer was confident, polished and young. He reminded me of Harry Hamilton with a few more years, better luck and the edge taken off.

"Help you, sir?" he asked politely.

"Early gold."

He spread his arms over the table. Everything was locked up in cases.

"Let me know if there's anything you'd like to see."

"Type One dollar," I said.

He bent to open the case.

"Charlotte, if you've got one."

The way he laughed, I knew right away Harry Hamilton wasn't fooling around, so I probed him about the coin market.

"Slabbed coins are the realm of the investor," he told me. "The real collector likes to feel the coin in his hand. Thinks *he* can judge a coin as well as the experts."

"So a slabbed Type One Charlotte dollar is kind of a strange entity?"

He nodded approvingly. "Spectacular and unobtainable."

"If I were interested in that kind of coin for my own portfolio, where would I go?"

He laughed. "I'd start at the bank."

"No problem," I said.

That stopped him cold. The quiet assurance of a third of a billion dollars sometimes has that effect on people, even when it's disguised by the likes of me.

He handed me a simple white business card.

"Let's talk soon," he said.

That afternoon I had a visit from a Pakistani green-grocer whose Brooklyn shop had been destroyed by a fire. The fire had been set by a deranged nine-year-old girl. Apparently the child had soaked a Cabbage Patch doll in gasoline, come in sucking her thumb and looking for chewing gum, and put the doll down in front of the space heater. Pretty intricate stuff for a nine-year-old mind, and a challenging case for the attorneys prosecuting for the insurance company. Nobody believed that the child harbored malicious intent, the jury had awarded nothing and the merchant was reduced to looking for a handout from me. He wanted sixty thousand and I gave it to him.

I was just putting away a Smith and Wesson catalog I'd received in the mail and preparing for the rush-hour drive home when a delegation from Kenya appeared downstairs.

"No delegations!" I raised my hands to Isabelle in a mock protective cross. "It's after five."

She gave me her stern look.

"Let them come back Monday," I groaned. "I want to take you home with me and eat wine-soaked raspberries off your stomach."

She gave me a hint of a smile. "You have to see them; it's about elephants."

"How badly do you want me to talk to them?" I asked slyly.

"How badly do you want those raspberries?"

Their leader was nearly seven feet tall and exuded the sort of raw physical power that came with being a generation away from loping across the plains. He spoke in Oxford tones.

"Have you ever seen an elephant up close, Mr. Dark?" he asked.

"In the zoo."

"Behind bars."

"No, in an exhibit with a moat."

"Like the human eye, the elephant eye relaxes to the horizon," he told me. "It's safe to assume that he feels no better about that exhibit than you would if you were the captive."

"I like elephants," I said. "You don't have to sell me on the fact that they're happier in the jungle. How can the Dark Foundation help you?"

He began to reel off figures about the decline in the elephant populations in East African parks. His men took out portfolio cases filled with ghastly pictures of elephant carcasses, killed for a few inches of ivory. He showed me a videotape of the slaughter of newborn elephants on the foundation's projection TV. It was too grisly for Isabelle to watch, and she left. I toughed it out.

"This is an economic problem, not an environmental one," I stated when his presentation was finished. "These poachers are starving. They kill elephants to feed their families. If the Dark Foundation contributes to your cause, their families will starve and the war will escalate and the elephants will die eventually anyway. You want Dark money for guns and patrols. I won't give it to you. Come back with another plan, one that takes into realistic account the economics of your country. Do that, and I'll give you as much as you can use."

The leader of the elephant delegation stared at me.

"I didn't expect to negotiate."

"Why not?"

"It's unusual to receive such a proposal from a philanthropic organization."

"I'll take that as a compliment."

"I meant it as one. We will come back with another plan."

"And details on how it can be monitored," I added.

He allowed me a tiny glimpse of his teeth and then he and his men were gone.

"Now can we get out of here?" I asked Isabelle.

Chapter 8

SHE FOLLOWED ME to Redding in her bright yellow
Mercedes-Benz 560SL convertible. The car had been
a Christmas bonus from the Dark Foundation, and Isabelle had protested terribly until I invoked the safety
issue. The foundation, I argued, could not afford to
have her lose any work time as the result of an accident, and a lesser car simply wouldn't do. Driving the
car was, she finally allowed, the price of being indis-
pensable.

The sun was almost gone by the time we reached
the top of the long driveway to the Redding house.
I have a theory that, much as the day sky is blue because it reflects the ocean, the dusk sky is greenish
because it reflects the leaves. My house was surrounded by a blue-green, almost metallic aura. I
turned off the SHO and sniffed the air.

"We should see deer," Isabelle breathed.

"Tolstoy's probably scared them all away."

"I hate that dog sometimes."

She went in while I retrieved him from his tether.

"Leave him out," Isabelle commanded.

"He's been alone all day."

"Trust me on this; you won't be sorry."

I rechained him and then went upstairs and ran the shower while Isabelle rummaged in the kitchen. I waited for the water to get hot and contemplated my good fortune.

As I've gotten older, sex has become more complicated, more intricate and more multidimensional. At least it has since I met Isabelle. Before I met her, I was never aware of how erotic the inside of an elbow can be. Before I met her, I had never stared into a woman's eyes while I climaxed. There were other things I hadn't done, too.

When she came to me in the shower, it was bit by bit: first a hand through the gap in the opaque shower door, then a wrist, then the elbow and the luscious patch of smooth skin inside it. I nibbled at her gently and pulled the rest of her in.

Isabelle works out a lot. When she's not giving money away and administering the Dark Foundation, she's most likely to be found taking, or teaching, a dance class.

"Hey," she said as I touched between her legs with the soap. "I'm not getting cheated out of a good dessert wine just because you have the patience of a tapir in heat."

"A tapir?"

"A wild pig."

I grinned at her and shampooed her head instead. She closed her eyes. When I was finished, I washed the rest of her, chastely, running the soap over the ultrafine blond hairs that cover her body. Those hairs make me crazy.

I reached to turn off the shower, but she stopped me.

"You kidding me?" she said. "I haven't even gotten started."

She took the soap bar from my hand and worked up a lather on my chest. Then she moved down.

"Raspberries," I croaked.

"Too planned. Where's your spontaneity?"

"But a fine plan! An outstanding plan!"

Sometimes Isabelle is like a train on rails. She just won't change direction. Sometimes I'm glad.

Later her thick blond mane spilled deliciously down her back and onto the top one of the towels from the heated rack. I propelled her gently to the bedroom, my hands on her hips from behind.

The bedroom in the Redding house is my favorite room in any of the Dark Foundation houses. The ceiling is a full fourteen feet, festooned with hanging plants nourished by huge skylights, full-spectrum fluorescent lighting and an automatic watering system. The room is sparsely furnished because the cavernous walk-in closets keep everything out of sight, but there is a cherry wood king-sized four-poster in the middle of the room and a long matching bench on which rests a British high-fidelity system. The wine and raspberries were already waiting by the bed: Isabelle's work. Now, they were just dessert.

I laid her gently on the bed and switched on Robert Cray.

"Oh, Nestor," she murmured. "What are we going to do with us."

"A lot more of this, I hope," I said as she took my head in her hands. "We're both specialists in giving it away with no strings attached."

"Threads, though," she said. "Definitely threads."

Chapter 9

IT WAS SATURDAY morning, and I awakened gradually, Isabelle's leg reassuringly heavy on mine, wondering what the hell I was doing with Harry Hamilton and why I was ignoring the advice of Charlie Bender. I slipped out of bed, pulled on a pair of sneakers, jeans and a T-shirt and went to feed Tolstoy. It was muggy and gray and threatening outside, and the house smelled of damp leaves.

While Tolstoy ate in his usual spot in the garage, I opened the closet, moved the shovels and brooms and rakes aside and pulled the false wall forward to reveal row after row of handguns, shotguns and rifles, so hidden as to discourage an inadvertent act of domestic violence. I figured that between Tolstoy's teeth and my hands and feet, I'd get to the garage if I really needed a gun.

I selected a Kimber 82 Cascade for the morning's outing. The Cascade is arguably the finest production sporting rimfire in the world, but I treasured it more because Uncle Andrew had given it to me than be-

cause it was the best of the .22s. Andrew Dark didn't
think much of me being a policeman, and he thought
even less of guns, but when he went to get me a gift,
he wanted one that would please *me,* not him, and he
did his homework and spared no expense. That's how
he was.

I pulled the Kimber, some paper and some shells
from the rack. Tolstoy looked woefully at the few
droolings left in his food dish and trotted after me.
We climbed the hill at the back of the property until
we reached the depression I had bulldozed to contain
noise and errant shells. I clipped a target onto the
backstop I'd set up there while Tolstoy marked every
inch of the hill as his own.

Ever since my days at the police academy, I have
used a firearm the way some people use a Ouija
board. Merely pressing the stock to my cheek acti-
vates an altered state of consciousness, one in which
words and thoughts and feelings flow through me
like an ebbing tide, gradually receding until I am left
alone in a silent universe of anticipation to be delivered by my own cosmic boom.

So I stood there on the gray-morning hill, framing
the tiny black ball in the match peep sight, breathing
in and out and asking myself who I was without all
of Uncle Andrew's money and wondering should I
follow the draw to the underbelly again; surround
myself with people on the make, lying people, cheating people, stealing people, killing people. I wondered whether my split-second edge was still sharp
enough for that, or whether I was better, and safer, in
the comfortable world of Dark money.

I squeezed off round after round, the tranquility between shots seducing me into losing track of time. At
one time I saw the center of the paper, surgically re-

moved by a ring of perfectly aimed shots, drop from the target and flutter aimless and limp to the ground in the faintest breeze. I saw myself piling out of the SWAT van, I saw myself running after street punks, my black shoes tapping the pavement, my knees high, my breath coming in huffs. I saw the panorama through the windshield as I bore down behind car after car after car in the fast lane during a high-speed chase. I saw hand-to-hand combat, too, with drug-crazed boys and flint-eyed pros. And I saw dinners with champagne and caviar, under chandeliers, and white gloves, and silk dresses, and I smelled perfume.

Her perfume.

"Hold your fire, cowboy," Isabelle called. "I'm coming up the hill."

A moment later she appeared beside me, sleepy, rumpled and luscious in my bathrobe.

"You're one hell of an alarm clock," she said.

"You were sleeping so soundly I didn't think you'd hear."

"Right," she said. "I always sleep through the sound of gunfire outside my window. Anyway, I have a breakfast suggestion."

"Go on, I'm hungry at the thought."

"Here's a hint. The first course involves raspberries and cream. . . ." She beckoned seductively with one svelte, painted finger, and I went to her as surely as I knew I would have to go to Harry Hamilton.

Chapter 10

In my first few years without parents, Uncle Andrew's light hand on my reins kept me off drugs and out of trouble, but it didn't fill my empty hours. I was curious about a lot of things, and I got in the habit of satisfying my curiosity by studying furiously and compulsively, devouring facts and opinions like food.

Annoying though it may be to my friends, my ravenous approach to life has surely helped the Dark Foundation. The "till" has swollen as much as it has, not because I am the world's most savvy investor, but because I'm not. I have never put a nickel of Dark money into something I didn't understand, and I didn't understand coins. If I were to find Harry Hamilton's counterfeiter, and if I were to find a new and lucrative investment vehicle for the foundation, I needed to teach myself from the bottom up.

So I spent Wednesday at the Metropolitan Museum of Art, roaming through glass cases full of ancient artifacts, trying to understand the nature of money. There was an exhibit of the first known coin, something called a Lydian Stater. There were also coins from the ancient states of Panticapaeum, Greece and Rome. Standing in front of the exhibit, I yearned to touch the coins, to hold them in my hand as people had thousands of years ago. When I could fight the urge no longer, I went to the museum offices and announced myself to one of the curators, a young man in blue jeans.

"You're Nestor Dark?" he asked.

"You're not what I expected either."

He smiled ruefully. "I guess I thought you'd be older, more formal. Anyway, I'm sorry I stared. How can I help you, sir?"

"I'm developing an interest in numismatics."

"I hope for our sake that this doesn't mean you're giving up your interest in Japanese porcelain."

I assured him that my interest in coins would have no impact on the continued growth of the Oriental antiquities collection in the Dark Wing, and two armed security guards accompanied us downstairs for a closer look at the coins I had been admiring. Onlookers strained for a look as we stepped over a section of purple velvet rope. The curator opened the case, reached in and handed me a Roman tetradrachmon. It felt cool and heavy in my hand.

"There was no mint in those days," the curator explained. "Each one of these coins was struck using a mallet and a hand-held die."

"Must have been easy to counterfeit."

He shook his head. "The dies themselves were specially cut by hand and resembled a punch with a unique design on the end. They were locked away each night, and if anyone was found tampering with them, the penalty was a swift death."

After I was finished at the museum, I used my portable phone and called the rare-gold dealer I'd met at the coin show. He remembered talking to me, and was suitably embarrassed when he learned my name. I accepted his offer of lunch at La Grenouille.

I've always been amused by a French restaurant that calls itself The Frog, but I have to admit that although trendier restaurants come to New York, and go, none ever offers food as consistently superb.

I may prefer to travel on two wheels or in my Ford SHO, but there are times and occasions where I must bring the full pomp and circumstance of being Nestor Dark to bear. Lunch at La Grenouille was such an occasion, and required a call to Isabelle.

"Have Waku meet me outside the Metropolitan Museum with the Benz."

"He's taking some contracts to the bank."

"He can do it later. I need him now. And, Isabelle?"

"Yes?"

"I need him dressed."

"Great," she said.

I hung up, thanked the curator and went to await my limousine on the front steps of the museum. It was a beautiful day for people-watching, and I tried to match the rhythm of passing footsteps with the snapping of the flags above me. The smell wafting up from the Sabrett hot dog vendor at the curb was making me crazy, tiny episodes of airborne torture with every cracking of his little steel lid.

"Come on, Waku," I murmured.

Five minutes turned into ten. Ten minutes into fifteen. It's not really Waku's fault that he's always late and hates to wear a uniform. Tribal aborigines often don't wear watches these days, and the most you're likely to see around their necks is war paint. A business suit can be a real problem.

Fifteen minutes turned into twenty, and I couldn't stand it anymore. I made a break for the hot dog stand, taking the vast steps of the Metropolitan two at a time.

"Gimme sauerkraut on a roll," I told the vendor. "Plenty of mustard."

"You kiddin' me?"

"I'm serious. No dog. Just the bun, mustard and the 'kraut."

"I don't sell sauerkraut," he said flatly, slamming the lid down on the delectable, brewing cabbage.

"I'm a vegetarian," I said, not wanting to admit that although I made exceptions, I wouldn't for a hot dog. "I have it all the time."

He looked me up and down.

"Gonna cost you the same," he said.

The steam from the cart was going directly to my face, and my salivary glands were working overtime.

"Now come on," I said.

At that moment, Waku pulled up in the stretched Mercedes-Benz 600. He leaped out and was between me and the cart in an instant, snatching the money from my hand.

"Hey!" said the hot dog man.

"He told me not to let him do this," Waku explained apologetically.

"I already put mustard on the roll!" I heard the man yell as the door slammed shut and Waku sprinted for the wheel. Once inside the car, he looked at me in the mirror.

"All the money in the world does not change some people," he mumbled.

"Goddammit Waku, it was only sauerkraut!"

He shook his head and floored the Benz. We left the curb with smoking tires. "Where to, Detective?"

All the time in the world doesn't change some people, either. Waku still calls me "detective" even though I haven't been a policeman for five years. He got into the habit when I collared him for running girls and turned him into the best street informant the NYPD ever had. I thought Rignola, my SWAT captain, was going to drill *me* with a sniper rifle when I took Waku off the street and gave him a job driving for me.

"You're not on the street no more, so you don't need that pimp for a chauffeur!" Rignola had railed.

"He's the best tracker I've ever seen, plus there's nobody with reflexes like him. I figure that should be worth something behind the wheel."

"Goddammit, Dark, he's worth more than that on the street. Leave him there!"

I took him and made my peace with the department later.

"La Grenouille," I told Waku. "I'm late."

He loves it when I tell him I'm late. He figures an ex-cop won't get a traffic ticket, and he's mostly right.

"I'm so happy I could turn into a chocolate drop," he said. "Then maybe some beautiful lady would scoop me up, or scrape me up, or if I was really lucky, suck me up."

Waku loves chocolate.

He greased the big Benz through the heavy Fifth Avenue traffic as if the three-ton limousine were some tiny, shiny pinball and he was at the flippers, and got me to lunch so fast I was no more than fashionably tardy.

The coin dealer was already seated and sipping a Perrier when I entered the restaurant to the usual fanfare.

"John Lion," he said, jumping up to greet me with a Wall Street flourish.

"That explains the flag above your coin table," I said.

He smiled, slightly embarrassed. "It's corny, but it works. You remember it, after all."

We ordered asparagus soup, and he began to talk.

"I'm sorry I didn't recognize you at the show. . . ."

"No problem," I said. "Lots of people don't recognize me. I like it that way. I'm not a movie star."

"I take it you're interested in starting a portfolio?"

"At this point, I'm interested in learning about coins."

"Is this for you personally, or for the Dark Foundation?"

"I am the Dark Foundation," I replied calmly, spooning my soup.

"Of course, of course. Silly of me. It's just that there are certain tax arrangements that can be made. . . ."

"I'm only interested in early gold."

"Hard to find," he said.

"That's why I'm interested."

He smiled. "I'd like to earn your business, Mr. Dark. If it's investments you're after, I can put together a portfolio of early coins—"

"I may ask you to do that for me," I said, "but right now I'm interested in another one of these."

I pulled Harry Hamilton's Charlotte dollar out of my pocket and put it on the table. Lion made a great show of pulling out his eyeglasses, wiping them with a handkerchief and fitting them to his ears and nose so perfectly that a carpenter with a micro-level would have been hard pressed to find a flaw.

The waiter brought some wine, but Lion was too absorbed to notice.

"This is a great numismatic rarity, Mr. Dark. May I ask where you got it?"

"It belongs to a friend of mine. I was hoping you could tell me where I could find another."

"The only man I know who can help you with this sort of coin lives in California," he said. "His name is Michael Pinipaldi, and he's very, very expensive."

He handed the coin back to me and I slipped it into the vest pocket of my blazer. He raised his wineglass.

"A toast to your interest in numismatics," he said. Then he smiled wryly. "And to some Dark money coming into the market."

Chapter 11

I WOULD HAVE left for Santa Barbara the next morning, but Isabelle had rearranged my schedule.

"But we already give to Brazilian famine," I protested.

"A hundred and ninety-seven thousand last year, and less than a fifth of that went to starving people. Nestor, it's disgusting how crooked these organizations are. The fat cats come to America for our money and take it home to buy limos, while their people starve. Now, the guys waiting outside are the genuine article, leftovers from the hippie era, really. They fly in over the bush and drop the food in parachutes. No accounting, no office, no nothing. They just take our money, load the plane and drop the food."

They turned out to be twins. They had the same green bush jackets on, the same work shirts, the same heavy dark eyebrows that joined in the middle and the same huge nose. One wore brown Bally weaves, the other black. Their shoes didn't go with the rest of their outfits. My once-over completed, I got right to business.

"Gentlemen, I'm Nestor Dark. Ms. Redfield informs me that you two drop food to starving people in Brazil. May I ask why?"

"Why?" the twin in black shoes repeated.

"That's right. I'm curious why you do it."

"Because nobody else will," he replied.

"I was in the Peace Corps down there," volunteered the other twin.

"We have already checked your references. Would you just give me the drill?"

"You give us the money, we buy the food, we fly it over the villages we know are the neediest, we drop the food. Simple," said the twin in black shoes.

"Is that the way you usually do it?"

"Sure," he replied.

"Well, we're going to do things a little bit differently this time. We will take care of buying the food, and we'll have it delivered directly to your airplane. We'll even have it loaded. Your fee will be based on the estimated value of previous runs minus the costs we incur. You'll get paid to fly. Regular bush pilot fees. There will be an observer from the foundation along."

"Wait a minute," protested the twin in black shoes. "We're a turnkey operation. Soup to nuts. No observers."

"We're just saving you some time and money," I replied.

"Uh-uh, no way. You give us the money, the food gets dropped. That's the way we always do it."

I could smell his nervous sweat.

"You've heard my offer."

"Please, man, we need the money," the other man wailed, decompensating completely.

"I'm offering you a fair fee," I answered.

"No dice," said the man in black shoes.

"Show the gentlemen out, would you please?" I asked Isabelle in my iciest tone. "We'll find another way to contribute."

Their expressions turned ugly, but I stared them down. When they were gone, Isabelle came back looking sheepish. I waved my hand, but that didn't stop her.

"They seemed so honest," she said. "So revolutionary."

"Usually you're very savvy. I'm surprised they got as far as they did. Maybe you're partial to hippies."

"Everyone's partial to hippies," she said. "They're so like children."

"Children don't wear three-hundred-dollar shoes," I said, and went to visit Aunt Unity.

Unity wasn't Uncle Andrew's wife, but the way she loved him, she might as well have been. Not marrying her was just one of his foibles, because he always went back to her. Always. And so did I, after my parents died, and long before the days of the Dark Foundation.

Uncle Andy didn't tell her when he was sick, and he made me swear not to, either. In the end he provided for her, but not enough. He just had this thing about blood and money. So I made up the difference. I knew he'd have wanted me to.

Uncle Andrew had conducted his grand affair with Unity in the classy Park Avenue duplex he'd rented for her. I'm a man of the road, a man drawn to change and challenge, but Unity is one of those people so deeply rooted in her surroundings that she looks small and frail when she's anywhere else, as if some of her body parts are missing.

After my uncle died, I bought her the apartment. It has a winding staircase, and the elevator opens on either the eleventh or the twelfth floor. Unity likes to descend to her guests, so I always ask to be taken to the eleventh. I have a suspicion—fueled by the glances of her elevator men—that she still entertains lovers up top. Even at fifty she could blast a man's trousers right off.

"You're sweet to think of me," she said, stepping off the staircase and into my arms. "I'm so glad I happened to be here."

That's our little game. She always says that. She knows I'm always thinking of her, and I know she's always at home.

Unity fancies herself an enchantress. She always smells like musky herbs and flowers, and every room is filled with books and occult artifacts of primitive belief systems. We sat on the couch in her cluttered, dimly lit living room and cleared the coffee table. Pynchon, the butler, came in with pâté and crackers. He's almost as big as Amos. I wonder about his relationship with Unity, but I've never said anything.

"How do you do it?" I shook my head and took a bite. "Stay so thin on pâté and crackers."

"I never eat pâté," she said.

I caught Pynchon's eye and winked, but as usual his expression didn't vary at all. He just looked right through me. I'm not sure I've ever heard him string a whole sentence together. That's why I figure he must be good for something else.

"You eat it all the time," I told her.

"Only when you're here."

"It's a spell, isn't it? A thin spell?"

She smiled as she got up and walked over to a beautiful, soccer-ball-sized pink orb.

"What do you think of my new crystal?" she asked. "It's rose quartz. It draws love."

"It's driving me crazy," I said, and took another bite of pâté. "Where'd you get it?"

She blushed with pleasure. "Downtown. A rock shop in Soho. Don't you think it's a beautiful addition to my collection?"

"Absolutely."

"Will you let me read your cards?"

I'm no expert on the Tarot, but I've seen a few packs, and so far, Unity's cards are unique. She tells me that they're one of a kind. They're beautifully drawn in an Egyptian motif with English titles. The edges are a bit frayed, but the artwork is exquisite. She pulled them out from beneath a purple pillow.

"Question of the day?" she asked.

Usually I have to think about this, but today I'd come prepared.

"Where will the search for false money lead?"

"Shuffle the cards."

I took them and shuffled them and returned them to her. Silently, she laid out ten cards.

"You have money on the brain," she said when she had finished. "Let's find out why."

"I know why."

"That's what you think," she said, overturning the first card. It was the "offering."

"I'd say it means assistance from a powerful person," she told me.

"Uncle Andrew," I replied, taking another bite of

pâté. She smiled wistfully enough for me to get a brief glimpse of what they'd had.

The second card was "generosity."

"In your case, prosperity," she said.

The third card was "dissension."

"Obstacles," she said.

"I've had 'em before." I picked up my teacup.

The fourth card showed the "weaver," an Egyptian woman bent to a loom.

"Attention to perfection in the creation of an object of beauty," said Unity.

I put my teacup down.

The fifth card showed the "navigator."

"Hidden enemies who must be vanquished," said Unity. She looked up at me. "Are you up to something, Nestor?"

"Mmm."

The sixth card showed the "prodigy." Unity interpreted it as a "painful lesson that will eventually bring benefit."

The seventh card showed the moon. I've always liked the moon. Unity shook her head. "Mystery," she said.

The eighth card showed the sun, and Unity's interpretation surprised me. "Love," she said. I rolled my eyes.

The ninth card made me lose my appetite completely. It showed a pillar destroyed by a bolt of lightning and two bodies falling from the sky. Unity didn't like it much, either.

"The obelisk," she said. "Havoc, ruin, a sudden event that destroys trust. Nestor, what have you gotten yourself into?"

"The usual," I said. "Let's see the last card."

It was "magnificence," and it seemed to pacify Unity. "You'll manage the situation," she said. "You always do."

But all I could think about was havoc and ruin.

Chapter 12

THE NEXT DAY I met Harry Hamilton at a Thai restaurant for lunch.

"So you've decided to be your own man again, huh?"

"Don't push your luck, Hamilton. I'll go as far as I feel like going with this."

"But doesn't it feel good to be back in the hunt?" he pressed.

"I went to the museum today, talked to the curator of numismatics," I replied.

"I told you I'd teach you everything you had to know," he said, using his bandaged hand to bring a large spoonful of chicken coconut soup to his mouth.

"There's just something about me," I said. "I'm better at teaching myself."

He lowered his voice. "Museum numismatics won't land you the counterfeiter," he said, "and it won't make you money in coins either."

"But the ultimate market for coins has to be collectors. It can't hurt to learn what they know. Anyway, this is how I do things. It's my style."

"Have you made any progress at all?"

"I've found a dealer in Santa Barbara who specializes in early gold. I'm going to see him in a few days."

Hamilton nodded thoughtfully.

"Makes some sense, I guess. Lots of old money there. The auction house that sold me the dollar does a lot of business with California."

"Don't you need to know the provenance of a coin like this?"

Hamilton shook his head, a half-smile on his face. "One doesn't always *want* to know how a coin came to market."

That made some sense to me.

"Then I'm off to the West Coast," I said.

"Oh no you're not," Isabelle said later that day. "You've got three meetings this afternoon."

"I'm flying away."

"You can't! One of them is an AIDS group. They say they've got a vaccine."

"Have they been to the National Institutes of Health?"

"NIH won't give them a dime. They say they're overextended as it is."

"Did you call and check on their story, their credentials?"

"You telling me how to do my job?"

"Who else is coming in?"

"A lady from the Parks Commission. She wants to plant a fern garden in Central Park with foundation money."

"A fern garden? Ferns can't take a New York winter."

"She wants to put them under a plastic bubble and have speakers playing Mozart to calm the unruly masses."

"I won't see her. She's obviously out of her mind. Who else?"

"A representative from the Scandinavian Federation. It's a joint Danish, Norwegian and Swedish group."

"I'd never have guessed. What do they want?"

"They've brought a Viking warship over from a Copenhagen museum, but they've run out of money to reassemble it and display it in Central Park."

"Ferns in Central Park, Viking boats in Central Park; what's going on here?"

Isabelle looked embarrassed.

"I try to group things like this together for you, so you can consider their relative merit."

"They have no merit. We're not in the park business."

"I thought after the Utah land. . . ."

"That's different. That's rattlesnakes. They haven't got any other friends. No commission or federation to help them. Reschedule the AIDS guys for next week, and in the meantime send the data on their research to Charlie Bender. The usual cover letter, I need your help on this one, blah blah blah."

"All this so you can go joyriding!"

She stormed out before I could tell her that I had some letters to do. That was probably for the best, since dictation remains an active and unresolved issue between us. It's really simple. I need someone to take dictation, and Isabelle refuses to do it. I've offered to pay to have her learn shorthand, but she's snubbed me, telling me that someone who earns a hundred and fifty thousand dollars a year shouldn't have to take letters. I agree, and have tried to hire a secretary for her, but she refuses to have another employee in the office. We have achieved an uneasy truce through the use of the dictating machine.

About the Starship, however, no peace is to be had. My high-tech turboprop remains the only issue that has nearly torn me and Isabelle asunder. Isabelle feels that buying such an extravagant toy is not in the spirit of Uncle Andrew's request, which shows how little she knows of Uncle Andrew. I spend all day, every day giving my money away, so I refuse to allow her to let me feel guilty about spending the money on the plane. Especially since it was purchased with such a wizardly combination of financing and tax credit that I have yet to pay for it.

I used the dictating machine for three letters to banks and brokers and then went to her office to say goodbye.

"I'll see you," I said.

"If you're lucky," she replied.

Chapter 13

THE PATH TO the Beechcraft Starship began before SWAT with the hot pursuit of a brutal rapist. I had him cornered at the end of the hall, and went for a tackle. In desperation he threw himself through a window and out onto the fire escape. I scraped past shards of glass, stepped out onto the rickety iron platform, looking down to see where he had gone, and discovered I was afraid of heights.

Paralyzed on the catwalk, I clutched the cold, rusting metal with my bare hands, weaving back and forth in a kind of pathetic trance. The rapist got away, and my partner had to pry me loose and talk me off the ledge like a jumper. He was a good guy and never told anybody, but when a crack addict's knife slid past his vest and he lay dying on the sidewalk, he made me promise to get comfortable with altitude. Seems like dying people are always getting me to promise something.

I didn't have to worry about it until I got the sniper job with SWAT. A sniper afraid of heights is about as useful as a poker player with no hands, so I had to conquer my fear step by step, fighting the lump in my throat and the sharpness in my chest and never saying a word to anyone; taking rooftops and belfries and catwalks with equal aplomb.

Finally it was the strong grip of wanderlust that took me from conquering my fear of heights to eliminating it. Uncle Andrew's money gave me the sudden freedom to come and go as I pleased, and that freedom was too powerfully intoxicating to be constrained by airline schedules. I went to flying school in Bridgeport, Connecticut, and devoted myself to the study of engines and updrafts and downdrafts and Instrument Landing Systems. My first instructor was an oversexed lady flyer whose idea of handling the stick had nothing to do with flying. I progressed to membership in the mile-high club, and then on to a multi-engine instrument rating. I was hooked.

Waku waved to the security guard and rolled the Benz right up to the Starship. He opened the door to the airplane and pulled the stairs down. While I went through my preflight check, Waku went through the inside of the plane, vacuuming and dusting the tables and windows until everything sparkled. Then he went outside and systematically checked the outside of the aircraft for loose nuts and bolts and other problems just as I had done a few minutes before. Waku comes from a culture that eschews technology, especially airplanes, believing that he and his people are capable of flying perfectly well without them. I used to laugh at this, but now, after some of the things I've seen Waku do, it just gives me the same uncomfortable feeling I used to get in math class when I suspected that everyone around me understood the problem better than I did.

I bid Waku adieu and sat forward in the custom deerskin pilot's seat. The Starship has a cockpit worthy of its name, and the array of softly-lit ergonomically perfect controls urged me to start my takeoff checklist. The Starship is not a jet, but its tandem wings, pusher engines, composite fuselage and space-age electronics help it perform like one while requiring less gas and only one pilot; critical for me, because I like to fly solo.

As usual, everything checked out perfectly, and I called the tower to file my flight plan. I proposed an immediate southerly turn, then a turn west to head over Pennsylvania and Ohio before dropping down again over the southeastern tip of Missouri in order to miss the Chicago Traffic Control Area. It was pretty much a straight shot after that, cruising at thirty-three thousand, in clear weather with a fifty-knot tail wind.

Since conquering my fear of heights, takeoff has become my favorite part of flying. Other parts of the flight may titillate the intellect more, but there is nothing that so stirs my soul as departing the planet's surface in total comfort and safety.

Unfortunately, departing the New York TCA in the Starship was as frustrating as riding a thoroughbred tied to a grinding mill. There were too many aircraft around to allow anything other than a painfully slow, highly regulated ascent. As I climbed, I looked energetically about and strained my ears for any emergency instructions from the traffic controller. Soon the ride smoothed out and the flying grew glorious. The sky was that deep, radiant blue that only altitude can reveal, the air so thin one isn't even sure it's there, the clouds and landscape beneath drawn as softly as the lines in a lover's skin.

I was high over the bootleg of Missouri—my headphones resting on the clip in front of me and Bach's Goldberg variations filling the cockpit—when the light on the Starship's cellular phone flashed. I picked it up. It was Isabelle.

"Nestor?"

"It better be, it's Nestor's plane and Nestor's number."

"Where are you?"

"Just crossing into Arkansas."

"There's a problem with the rattlesnakes."

"What kind of problem?"

"The Park Service just called. They won't okay the release. They say there's no way that we can guarantee that the snakes will stay put."

Far below me I saw a golden eagle soaring easily, looking for mice. I craned to see him for longer, but he flashed beneath me like firefly in daylight and was gone.

"We've been through all this."

"I'm just telling you what they said. The Nature Conservancy called too. They want you to back down on the snakes."

I hung up and checked the charts for an unscheduled stop.

Chapter 14

BOTH ARKANSAS AND Santa Barbara lay well north of my new destination, and I had had to change course. I put my headphones back on and filed my revised flight plan with the tower at Little Rock, then veered in a gradual line that would take me just below Wichita, over the Continental Divide and the Uncompahgre Plateau and straight to the field at Moab, Utah.

I spent the remaining hours of the flight trying to regain the peace I had felt before Isabelle's call. My passion for flying overpowers my fear of heights because of the addictive serenity that being aloft holds for me. It separates me from the demands of the hordes who want Dark money, it separates me from the expectations of my friends, even Isabelle, and it allows me to get closer to my memories. I wouldn't want to stay high and out of touch forever, but breathing room is always welcome.

My reverie aloft came to an end when I checked in with Salt Lake City TCA and then with the tower at

Moab. There was no traffic, and I began my approach.

Moab is notable mostly for its proximity to both Arches and Canyonlands National parks. It is a field for small Cessnas and Piper Cubs. Few Beechcraft Starships land there. I circled long and low, watching the flashes of bright white light from my wingtips wash over the red desert floor. Most of Utah is the red of dried blood, as if some gigantic wound had opened up millions of years ago and gushed and gushed until it coagulated into the bumpy scabs called Arches and the deep fissures known as the Canyonlands.

Just before my wheels hit the ground, I closed my eyes and tried to extend my chi so that I could feel the ground with it. I cut the throttles, lifted the flaps and made a three-pointer to the dying whistle of the turboprops. There was no taxiing to do; I simply pulled the airplane off the runway and parked.

Schlieren rose from the tarmac in the Utah sun. I barely had time to run through the shutdown before the cockpit grew hot enough to make me sweat. I signed off with the control tower, finished the log and lowered the stairs just as three men approached the jet.

The first wore Park Service green, a side arm and a Stetson. The second man I presumed to be from the Nature Conservancy. Even from a distance I could see the concerned and furrowed brow of the conservation activist. The hot desert wind blew the tails of his inappropriate navy blue suit up high around his waist, keeping his hands constantly busy smoothing them.

The last man had too little hair and too much

stomach. He wiped his face repeatedly with a white handkerchief.

Between the pants-hitching and the forehead-wiping and the Stetson-adjusting, the three of them were a discordant symphony of motion, and they made haste to my plane.

The ranger offered his hand as I came down off the steps. It was a hard hand, but so was mine, and I could see that impressed him.

"Ranger Robinson," he said.

"We're so happy you could come at short notice," interrupted the fat man, slipping his pudgy hand into mine. "I'm Kales. Plateau Realty."

The man from the Nature Conservancy looked annoyed to have to expose himself to the sun, and annoyed to have to walk the distance from the terminal to the airplane in the company of the other two. He introduced himself as "Fitzwater of the Conservancy" and suggested we make haste back to the air-conditioning.

Kales suggested that we hold our discussions at the agency offices, but the other two didn't think much of that idea. I suggested the Dark Ranch, and we drove there in silence in Fitzwater's frigid black rental sedan.

Much as I love it, I don't use the ranch often, which was one of my primary reasons for deciding to give it up. It is situated along the high bank of the Colorado River, just north of the heart-shaped piece of land that comprises Arches National Park. The simple, modest outside belies an inside as lavish and charming as an Austrian lodge. In fact, much of the heavy, dark wood furniture was brought over from the Alps after what my uncle described as a "particularly romantic trip." The property is spectacular, but other than the caretaker and maid whom Kales's agency sends twice monthly, there is rarely anyone there to enjoy it.

I opened the door and let the others in. Kales and Robinson were impressed by the place and showed it. Fitzwater was impressed by the place and tried not to show it. I felt a terrible and unexpected sadness at the idea that soon this house would no longer be mine.

We sat down to talk at a long wooden table that looked like it came from a castle of Arthurian legend. Strange pink light from the red desert came in and cast shadows. I filled an espresso machine and made strong black coffee for my guests and ginseng tea for myself.

"I'm sure that we can reach some compromise on the rattlesnakes," Kales began.

I took a long sip, put down my cup and pointed a finger at Kales.

"First of all," I answered, "I'm not even sure why you are here, Mr. Kales. I don't recall asking you to be involved in this discussion. Did either of you ask Mr. Kales along?"

Fitzwater shook his head. Ranger Robinson also denied inviting Kales and gave me an almost imperceptible smile.

"I'm the listing agent," Kales sputtered. "I knew your uncle, I was involved in the purchase of the ranch, I—"

"My uncle is dead," I said. "And he was never involved in any of this anyway. I continue to be baffled as to why you are here. If you want to stay, please allow me to finish my business with these men. If we come to some agreement, you'll get your points for executing the transfer."

Kales looked at the other two for support, but

when none was forthcoming he wiped his brow one last time, not daring to bristle, and fell silent.

"About these snakes," said Fitzwater.

I held up my hand.

"This entire deal is about these snakes. The only reason I am willing to give up land I love, land that was in my family, is so that these snakes can forever have a place to procreate in peace. No snakes, no land. It's as simple as that."

Robinson shifted in his chair.

"May I ask why you have an interest in Klauber's rock rattlesnake?"

"Yes." Fitzwater leaned forward to catch the answer. "The Conservancy's been wondering that, too."

"For precisely the reason that you both find it so unbelievable," I replied. "Because nobody else does. They're endangered, they belong here, they were here before we were and I hope they will be here after we're gone, and I want to help them."

"But they're very deadly," said Robinson. "Small snake, big fangs, potent venom. And they like to hide in rock crevices. Just the kind of place a climber likes to put his fingers. A lot of people come out here to climb."

I asked Fitzwater if he'd ever seen a rock rattler, and he shook his head.

"They're not that easy to find," Robinson said.

"They are for me," I said and stood up.

I led the men out the back door of the ranch house and across the bluff toward an abandoned well. Once when I was a little boy, I had found a rock rattler there, draped it over my knee and stroked its head lovingly, never realizing the danger I was in. My father had found me there, killed the snake and systematically exterminated all the rock rattlers in the area, including a nest of babies just emerging from the egg.

"Magnificent view," said Fitzwater as we neared the edge.

"How far to the bottom?" Kales asked, peering over nervously.

"Three, four hundred feet," I answered.

A small pile of rocks marked the well. Kales hiked up his pants, as if it would help him see the ground better. Fitzwater strode purposefully. Robinson looked around alertly.

I used a stick to poke around until I felt a slight push of resistance; then I bent down and took an eye-level peek.

"Watch out," Robinson warned. I tilted back a rock that resembled a dinner plate, and she slithered out.

She was a mature female, and her colors were a bit faded with age, as if her hair had gone gray. But she was wrinkle-free as a new balloon, and the rest of her was as beautiful as her tiny black eyes. Fitzwater's fascinated expression pleased me.

"So they're already here," he said.

I nodded. "And I want them to stay here."

Robinson shook his head. "We just can't allow it. We're too close to parkland to start a snake farm."

"No snakes, no title," I said.

Kales wiped his forehead for the thousandth time. "Mr. Dark?"

I nodded.

"I have a suggestion. You don't look like you're too happy about parting with your ranch. And frankly, I don't see why you should. Why not keep the house and the land immediately surrounding it, say maybe fifty acres, and donate the land in the hills to the Nature Conservancy? I'm sure Ranger Robinson would have no objection, and while the Conservancy might have enjoyed having your beautiful ranch house, I'm sure they'll be happy with any land you give them."

It was so ridiculously simple. It had to be, for Kales to have figured it out. The snakes really didn't have to be by the well, and I didn't really *have* to give up the ranch, even if Isabelle thought I had too many homes.

"Fine with us," said Robinson.

Fitzwater's face showed that he was still stinging from the remark implying trysts, but he pulled himself together quickly enough. "If you insist on creating a refuge for the snakes," he said, "I suppose the Conservancy has no choice."

I was surprised at my relief, and surprised at Kales.

"That might just work," I said, smiling and thinking of Uncle Andrew.

The ranch was staying in the family.

Chapter 15

Although it blends the best of the two states of mind that are California—the cool, aloof cosmopolitan north and the seething, egotistically creative south—Santa Barbara has always been too motionless for me. It's a beautiful place to relax, but living there for any length of time makes me long to stir things up, something I was bound to do on this visit.

I left Moab and joined the dawn over the Pacific. Santa Barbara tower ushered me in, and I parked at my reserved tie-down. I walked out through the terminal carrying only a Halliburton overnight bag, and hailed a cab for the sloping ocean hillside Santa Barbarans refer to as the Riviera. It was here—amidst the pungent eucalyptus and beneath the faultless blue sky—that Uncle Andrew had built his last home. Although the local building ordinances dictated that it be white with an adobe roof, the house was a paragon of modernism, the only house in Andrew Dark's collection that might be considered sterile. When I first saw it, I disliked its cold white walls and empty rooms, but the more I learned about my uncle, the more I understood that he viewed his homes around the world as mirrors to his moods, and built them accordingly. The Santa Barbara house was for the cool, dispassionate Andrew Dark, and was therefore too neat and aloof for Isabelle. She despised it nearly as much as my airplane, and referred to it as The Hospital. I went there when I needed to think.

Isabelle was curt and distant when I called in, and claimed to have no messages she couldn't handle without me.

"You going to tell me what you're doing out there and why you've been so secretive lately?"

"I'm detecting," I said.

"What?"

"I'm doing some private investigating."

"Private investigating!"

"Don't worry, it won't interfere with foundation business. I'm just helping a guy out."

"I thought you gave up being a policeman."

"Goddammit, why does everybody say that to me!"

"I guess I'm sort of glad to hear that's what this is all about. I thought you had a girlfriend or something."

I reassured her that she was the queen of my days and then set out in Uncle Andrew's pearl-white Rolls Corniche convertible to pay the "very, very expensive" Michael Pinipaldi a visit.

Montecito—Santa Barbara's ritziest suburb—is commercially divided into upper and lower villages. I pulled the Rolls into the parking lot of a small shopping center in the upper village and walked down the cool path amidst carefully trimmed hedges and pueblo-like walkways covered in ivy. Tangible Scarcities was no more than a wooden door with a classy sign that bespoke old money. I hesitated for a moment before ringing the doorbell, thinking that Uncle Andrew would have felt far more at home here than I did.

The door swung silently open at the hand of a woman best described as a classic Spanish beauty. She had an aquiline nose, deep-set blue eyes, cheekbones that would have been the envy of any fashion model in the world, and lustrously thick raven hair. A single large sapphire set in a thick and flat gold chain clung to a smooth throat that tapered to a long, graceful neck. Her dress matched her eyes and showed off a riveting deep cleavage and full hips.

"May I help you?" she inquired.

"Mr. Pinipaldi," I managed. "I'm here to see Mr. Pinipaldi."

"And you are. . . ?"

The effect she had on me obviously amused her.

"Nestor Dark."

"Do you have an appointment, Mr. Dark?"

At that moment a man resembling nothing so much as a large black bear strode into the room.

"Mr. Dark doesn't need an appointment, Morgan," he told her. He offered his hand and we shook, an experience that I know infused me with at least an hour's worth of vital male essence.

"I'm Michael Pinipaldi," he said.

"I got your name from—" I began.

"John Lion. Yes, yes, I know. Although even without him, your reputation precedes you, Mr. Dark. I am nonetheless gratified to see that nothing in your vast business experience has completely prepared you for Ms. Morgan Pajaro."

His eyes crinkled into a smile as he nodded toward the beautiful young woman who had admitted me.

"Nothing in my *life* experience has prepared me for Ms. Pajaro," I said truthfully, flashing her a smile.

"I can certainly understand that." Pinipaldi beamed. "Before we get started, may I ask if I can help you with accommodations, reservations, anything of that nature?"

"I have a home here in Santa Barbara," I said.

The elegant Ms. Pajaro shot me a glance.

"Something to drink, then?" asked Pinipaldi.

"I'll have a beer, if you've got one."

"Budweiser, Corona, Carlsberg?"

"Carlsberg."

I sat in a plush chair near an empty glass display case while Pinipaldi rushed out.

"I'm surprised to hear you live here," said Morgan, sinking gracefully into the chair behind the case. "Perhaps we have some friends in common."

"If we had, I'm sure we would have met by now." I smiled at her. "I have a house on the Riviera, but unfortunately I don't spend enough time here."

The chauvinist in me was unnerved by the cool way she appraised me, but before I could comment on it, Pinipaldi rushed back in with a cold one.

"It's not true that rare coins are a universally sound investment," he announced without preamble, settling into the chair next to mine. "Coin dealers are fond of touting a certain study done by Salomon Brothers in New York. . . ."

". . . which ranks coins as the number one investment over a twenty-year period," I finished.

"Of course, you *would* be familiar with it. But you see, the study doesn't mean much. Lots of people lose money in coins. Far more than gain. Cheers."

He raised his own Carlsberg to mine and we toasted. When I turned to look at Morgan, she had gone, and Pinipaldi rose and took her place behind the case.

"Coins, indeed any collectible, perform remarkably like any other investment. If demand exceeds supply, they go up. If supply exceeds demand, they go down. There are other, complicating market forces at work, and when you begin to invest for your foundation, it will be my greatest pleasure to explore them with you, but for now the major point is that your success or failure with coins as an investment vehicle depends almost entirely on the coins you select."

"And that's where you come in," I said.

"Precisely." He grinned. "I know the right coins, and I can get them for you at the right price."

So saying, he bent to manipulate the display case between us, and suddenly the case was no longer empty, but revealed a tasteful array of small gold pieces.

"False bottom," he explained, holding up the red velvet liner.

"Ah."

"I am hoping that you will select me to help you develop a portfolio, but to be perfectly honest, I would rather that you selected me to help you develop a collection. You see, Mr. Dark, the greatest joy of numismatics is not to be found in the rate at which the coins appreciate, but in the coins themselves. Take these examples here."

"Very beautiful," I said.

Pinipaldi shrugged. "Their design? In my opinion, mediocre. But to the informed eye, Mr. Dark, they are beautiful beyond measure. Do you know anything of mints?"

"Fort Knox."

"A depository for gold reserves, not a mint. Mints are where coins are struck; physically manufactured. There have been eight mints in the history of United States coinage, although at the present time the only ones operating are in Philadelphia, Denver and San Francisco. What's interesting, though, is that out of all the coins minted by the United States government, only one series, the five-dollar gold piece, or half eagle, as it is called by numismatics, was minted in all eight mints. The half eagles you see in this case are the rarest of those coins, those minted—"

"In Charlotte, North Carolina."

Pinipaldi leaped from his chair and clapped his hands with joy.

"Right you are, Mr. Dark, and in Dahlonega, Georgia! You're a man who does his homework! These are tough coins to find, particularly in the pristine condition that they appear here. These are the kind of coins one needs to find and stash away if one wants to profit from numismatics. They are the true tangible scarcities, the coins that people who love coins would kill for!"

I knew the speech was well rehearsed—and delivered sans Morgan Pajaro for its full and undiluted effect—and it sounded like a fair con. It would take time for me to get to the bottom of it. Time for me to see some more of the breathtaking Ms. Pajaro.

Chapter 16

AFTER LEAVING TANGIBLE Scarcities, I drove the Rolls downtown and made a round of the local bookstores, picking up all the books on coins I could find. I spent the balance of the afternoon reading on the patio of Uncle Andrew's house, my chest bare to the warm Southern California sunshine, a mango iced tea by my side. I read a little bit more about mints and the gold pieces Pinipaldi had shown me, verifying the information he gave me and boning up for the next step in the plan.

At four-thirty, I went to the garage and fired up the great thumping Moto Guzzi motorcycle I kept there. It was a classic Italian bike, perfect for the canyon roads of Santa Barbara. The twin black tailpipes smoked black for a few minutes as it protested being awakened from a long sleep, but finally the engine settled down into a relaxed cadence, and I mounted up and headed for Montecito for the second time that day.

When I arrived at the familiar shopping center in

the upper village, I parked the bike inconspicuously and checked my watch. I had two minutes to spare.

Morgan Pajaro emerged alone from the ivy-covered walkway at precisely five o'clock. I was lounging against the weathered wood of an antique-clock shop.

"Somehow I knew you'd be the punctual type," I said.

"I didn't want to keep you waiting," she replied.

"That certain I'd be here?"

"Yes. Where's your Rolls?"

I looked impressed.

"I came out to the parking lot for a look while you were in with Michael," she admitted.

"On your own or for him?"

"On my own."

"Did you give him a report?"

"He didn't ask for one."

"How'd you know the Rolls was mine?"

"If a Rolls-Royce with the license plate 'DARK' belonged to someone else, it would have been a hell of a coincidence."

"Lots of light left for a bike ride," I said.

"Lots of dark left, too," she answered.

So I followed her home to put on some pants and a leather jacket. She lived in a small and trendy apartment complex on the west side. She made me wait outside while she changed, but I guessed the place had an ocean view as good as the one from The Hospital.

She emerged looking morning-fresh and filling a pair of jeans in felonious fashion. I supposed her job was not very strenuous, and I said so. She held my helmet in her hands for a moment and studied my face.

"Let's get one thing straight, Mr. Dark," she said. "Coins are very exacting work, and I'm no bimbo. I go to all the shows and do Michael's buying for him. I also help him grade the coins and make the rounds of estate sales looking for treasures."

I put up my hands in mock surrender.

"You're the coin pro, not me."

She climbed on the Guzzi behind me, putting a chaste distance between us, her hands resting lightly on my hipbones. The first time I put on the brakes, she pushed herself upright so as not to push me forward and over the handlebars. It was clear she'd ridden before, so I set out for one of the most scenic drives in the southland.

State Highway 154, known locally as San Marcos Pass, winds breathtakingly up and out of Santa Barbara. We reached the summit of the coastal range, then dropped into the Santa Ynez Valley, turning off onto Cold Springs Road: a mecca for bikers, diners and hikers alike, and home to Cold Springs Tavern.

I like the place even though I don't eat meat. It's warm, chummy, has excellent vegetables, and on most Sunday mornings features a fine selection of two-wheeled exotica. I found a spot in the hard-packed dirt and killed the big Guzzi. Morgan climbed off, removed the helmet I had lent her and shook her magnificent black mane back and forth until I thought my heart would stop.

"How'd you know about this place?" she asked.

"How do *you* know about it?"

"I have friends who ride," she answered. "And I like a big juicy steak now and then."

"First time I laid eyes on you I knew you were a meat-eater," I said.

We went inside and were told there was a wait for a table.

"Friday nights are always like this," Morgan announced. "We can get a drink at the bar."

Easier said than done. The place was packed with spilled beer, cigarette smoke and shoulders. I nosed my way through the crowds, Morgan's cool hand in mine, until I found a couple of spots at the bar. She ordered Lilet Blanc. I ordered coffee.

"What a man," she said.

"I don't drink and drive," I replied steadily, giving her my best stern and serious look. "Especially when I have to ride home at night on a motorcycle with a beautiful woman on the back."

The bartender slid us our drinks, and I asked her how long she had worked for Pinipaldi. She took long enough to answer for me to have a look around the bar and notice all the looks she was collecting.

"I met Michael three years ago at a hotel in San Francisco," she said. "He was helping a client up there. A representative for one of the larger European banks. I was just having a drink after a graduate school exam."

"Berkeley?"

"Stanford. I majored in American history."

"But you're not a native Californian?"

She shook her head. "My father was a Spaniard, my mother was Lebanese. They raised me in Madrid and then in Boston. By the time I finished a year at the Sorbonne and graduated from Radcliffe, I guess all my accents kind of melted together."

I gave a long, low, impressed whistle. She just smiled and lifted her Lilet.

"And Pinipaldi hired you because you could say all the presidents in order," I said.

She gave me a very hard look. "He hired me, Mr. Dark, because Michael and I have something very important in common. We both grew up poor, and neither of us wants to die that way."

Right at that moment, before I could even ask her to call me Nestor, two jokers showed up to take our seats.

This was the downside to the Cold Springs Tavern, and I'd experienced it before. Not all motorcyclists work an honest day, and although rare, the motor-cycling scumbag does exist, and does frequent the tavern and does drink too much and does come look-ing for one last bit of trouble before he makes a gooey red smear of himself on some mountain road.

"You took our seats," the two chorused gruffly.

"Truth is, we've been here for quite some time," I said, swiveling my stool around to face them.

"The seats were empty when we took them," said Morgan.

Both were big men with scraggly beards, leather vests, blue jeans and riding boots. One wore a red flannel shirt, the other blue, and they both had bellies busy busting out of their trousers. They each took ten eyefuls of Morgan.

"You can stay," the bad boy in blue told her. "He's got to move."

"Why don't you boys just take a walk and leave me and the lady in peace? There'll be somewhere else to sit down in a few minutes."

"Buy us a beer and we'll think about it," said the man in red.

"Buy your own," I said, sliding slowly off my stool. "Then take 'em outside until you cool off."

By this time we had an audience. The bartender appeared, and he looked worried.

"We're busy," he said. "Got no room for trouble. You two can wait till other seats open up."

Then the biker in blue made the mistake of slipping his arm through Morgan's.

"That's a damn good idea," he said. "Why don't the three of us just have our drinks outside?"

Morgan tried to pull away, and I ran out of patience and stood up.

There's a little spot at the base of the throat, a fleshy depression right above where the bones of the sternum meet. If you put two fingers in that spot and press inward and down, hooking over the bone, you encounter an exceedingly sensitive plexus of nerves. I reached out and stabbed the blue biker in precisely that spot, pushing down hard and bringing him to his knees. His friend was transfixed by the ease at which the bigger man yielded to me. I made sure to squeeze hard and fast, discouraging further argument and making the man's eyeballs extrude and his hands leap for mine in a desperate struggle for relief.

"We're not moving," I said quietly. "Go find someplace else to sit."

If the other man had stayed put, it all would have ended there, but he didn't. Galvanized into action by his friend's plight, he came at me quickly, shoving Morgan out of the way. Seeing her hit the edge of the bar pissed me off more, and I exploded with chi.

This is something one is not supposed to do in a bar. Chi is to be conserved, channeled, nurtured and used to promote health and well-being. The best parallel I can draw is between the peacetime and the wartime uses of nuclear power. Amos had been over and over this notion a hundred times, as had my previous teachers. Whether one viewed chi as a limitless power stemming from the very fabric of the universe or as an exhaustible bioelectric resource, there was no point in squandering it.

But squander it I did. I opened the meridians to my right leg and loosed a Wing Chun heel kick into the underside of my attacker's ribs. As soon as the foot made contact, I saw his face screw up in pain and disbelief, and he flew back across the room and slammed into the wall at the rear of the bar with sufficient force to go partway through the plaster. At the sound of his ribs cracking, I released the man at my feet, and he keeled over, grasping his throat.

By this time most everybody in the bar was on his feet and staring at me. I could hear my long, deep breathing in the silence. I put a hundred-dollar bill down on the counter to cover the damage, and took Morgan by the arm and led her gently outside.

The look in her eyes told me I'd be learning about more than coins that night.

Chapter 17

THE RIDE BACK down the hill and into town was distinguished primarily by the constant pressing warmth of Morgan Pajaro's body against my back and the decidedly clear message of her hand between my legs. The setting sun in my eyes, the treacherous curves of the road and my rising hormones conspired to make controlling the big Guzzi all but impossible, and I finally pulled off the pass at the crest onto a ridge road called East Camino Cielo.

I drove along the ridge for a while, until the road tightened down to a series of tight sandy switchbacks, filled with potholes and lined by sandstone formations. There were caves up here, long ago occupied by Native Americans and painted with dramatic scenes. The light was slowly fading, and the rays of the sun, filtered through the choked atmosphere of the southland, lit up the pale rocks in a dramatic pink wash. I backed off the throttle and eased the bike onto the shoulder.

Morgan swung her long leg over the back of the

bike and planted it down squarely in front of me, her hips jutting my way. She removed the helmet in a flash and shook her thick black hair until it sparkled like her eyes in the twilight. She was a vision, and she stepped closer and touched my lips with her hands.

"I've learned a lot about you in a short time, Nestor Dark," she said.

"What have you learned?"

"I've learned that you used to be a policeman. I've learned that you have a foundation and that you have loads of money. I've learned that you know how to use your hands and feet, that you go where you want and do what you want."

In response I took her by the hand and led her up a steep path to a cave mouth.

"There are rattlesnakes up here," she protested. "Don't you know that rattlesnakes like high ground?"

"I get along well with rattlesnakes," I answered, pulling her gently along until we reached the cave. It was nearly pitch black inside, and I ran my bike boot over the ground in sweeping strokes just in case her reptilian prognostications turned out to be correct. There was nary a rattle, and I turned and took her in my arms, framing us both in the portal and the light.

"What do you think of me, Mr. Dark?" she whispered, her lips brushing mine, her breath sweet with wine.

"I think you're a tease and I think you should call me Nestor."

She ran her hand gently over my bulge, fluttering her fingers like butterflies. It was clear she'd done it before.

Then she pulled away coyly.

"I really want to know," she said. "What do you think of me?"

"You're a magnificent woman," I said. She gave me a look that said she was looking for something more original.

"And I think you're bored, and I think you're angry," I continued.

"Go on."

"You know what you do to men, that's for sure, and I think you've been flattered so long that you're bored with them telling you they want to sleep with you and you're angry that there isn't anything else."

She sat down and I sat down beside her.

"Why did you come to the gallery?"

"I have a couple of friends who've made some money in coins and I thought I should look into them as a potential investment for the foundation."

"What do you care about investments?" she asked bitterly. "You've got more money than you could possibly spend. Why don't you just let some bank run the thing and go have fun?"

"I do have fun," I said, taking her slender white hand in mine. "I enjoy giving money away and helping people, and if I want to keep doing that, I have to make sure that the Dark Foundation retains its capital. We only give away profit; that way we can keep the machine running. Even so, you'd be surprised at the fun I have."

She edged closer to me.

"Michael wants me to sell you," she said.

"Now that's a surprise."

"It's very important to him. He'd have me do almost anything. He's not a nice man."

With that she leaned up and kissed me hungrily on the lips. "You were so sexy at the bar," she murmured into my mouth. "The way you took care of those guys."

"I didn't enjoy it. They needed taking care of, that's all," I responded, moving my mouth to the wispy hairs around her ear.

"You sure that was all?" She took my hand and put it on her breast.

I was overcome there in the cave. Overcome by the excitement of the strange setting, overcome by her exotic beauty, her musky perfume, her perfect skin, the tantalizing way she ran her fingers lightly over mine. I gave in and unbuttoned her blouse and slipped my hands in and around her back, clasping her to me and unfastening her bra at the same time.

When I looked up from her chest, I saw that her eyes were closed and her head was thrown back. I kissed her gently on the throat and then I moved down to take her nipples in my mouth and slip my hand into her jeans. She moaned and tried to wriggle out of them without taking her hands from the back of my head, where they were gluing my lips to her bosom. I felt her wetness, and I heard her heart start to race and I thought about what she had said about Pinipaldi wanting her to sell me and I stopped moving and I pulled away.

The air in the cave was dank and chilly, and the ground was covered with uncomfortable small stones.

"We really should be getting back to business," I said, rising and helping her up. "Michael really wants you to sell me."

She brushed the dust from her jeans and hurried out of the cave, buttoning her blouse and not meeting my eye.

We remounted the Guzzi in silence and roared off to rejoin the pass. Morgan stayed as far back as possible, making only the most necessary physical contact. Once back at sea level, I took the freeway downtown and pulled up in front of her apartment. She handed me her helmet.

"I wish you hadn't told me I was a sales project," I said.

It's not often that someone catches me with a blow to the face. When you have practiced the martial arts long enough, the responses become ingrained, innate enough to galvanize you into action regardless of the circumstances or your state of mind. Years of training notwithstanding, Morgan's hand stung my face. Maybe my reflexes were on standby so that I wouldn't hurt her. Maybe.

"That was for making me feel like a whore," she said. Then she turned on her heel and strode up the driveway to her complex.

Of course I went after her. With her helmet dangling from one arm and mine from the other, I gunned the big Guzzi after her, pulling it around and blocking her retreat just before she reached the stairs.

"You're lovers, aren't you?" I demanded. "You and Pinipaldi?"

"None of your goddamn business." She tossed her head and picked up the pace. I stayed with her up a flight of outdoor stairs and to the door of her apartment.

"So what else have you found out about me?" I said as she stepped inside.

"How little you know about women," she answered, and closed the door in my face.

I stood there for a time, my face stinging in the cool Santa Barbara night. Finally I knocked on the door. There was no answer, and I couldn't find a doorbell, so I knocked again. More insistently this time. A full five minutes went by and she finally answered the door, wearing a ruby silk bathrobe that matched her perfectly painted toes.

"I'm sorry," I said.

"You should be."

"May I come in?"

She seemed reluctant, but she stood aside.

Her apartment was not so different from the painted cave, and I was right about the view. It was perfect. The furnishings were vintage Santa Fe, and the walls bore numerous pen-and-ink sketches which I inspected while she poured herself some wine at the wet bar.

"Are these your work?"

"Do you like them?"

"Very much. Whoever drew them is comfortable with the starkness and the angles of nature. They're sad, but beautiful, like you."

"They're mine. Drink?"

"I can't," I said. "I've got the motorcycle." I wandered over to the bar.

"What's your poison when you can?"

"Bourbon."

"Turkey or Daniels?"

"Ezra Brooks."

She took out a bottle of Wild Turkey and poured me a stiff one over ice.

"If I drink this, I can't ride home," I said, taking the glass.

"Then I guess you can't ride home," she replied, gravely, giving me the tiniest hint of a smile.

The apartment had a loft, and she led me to it, drinks in hand. I linked my fingers, stained slightly brown from my leather motorcycle gloves, with her finely painted ones as we climbed, my chest even with her delicious rear.

She had a futon bed, Japanese style, low to the ground and hard as the cave floor, but a lot cleaner and pebble-free.

"What made you change your mind?" I mumbled as she took me in her arms and dropped her robe.

"You're not the only one who does what they want to do," she said, unbuttoning my shirt.

I put my hands flat against her belly and then slid them down and around to press her to me. Her musky smell came to me again, mixed with the cinnamon of mouthwash that told me she knew she I was going to stand outside and she knew she was going to let me in all the time. I hated to be so easy, but she was so glorious in her nakedness that she made me forget all sorts of things for the second time in a day.

Morgan Pajaro had a Latin appetite for love. I tried to be tender, but she rode me like a Castilian cowgirl, her thighs bunched under her, driving me up to the edge and then suddenly back down whenever she felt me grow tense. She did this to me several times, until she couldn't wait any longer and she came in a long wail, her head thrown back as when she had proffered her throat, her arms on my chest and stiff and triangulated, locked against me so that, for minutes, I couldn't get my mouth to hers.

While she rested, her head on my chest, she asked me if there was a woman in my life.

"Yes and no," I answered.

"Ever been married?"

"Never."

"Does the yes-and-no live in California?"

"New York."

"Would she mind that you're with me?"

"Yes, she would."

"Do you feel guilty?"

"Not a bit," I lied, and stroked her hair.

Chapter 18

THAT FIRST NIGHT with Morgan was full of murmurs and moans, ecstasy and anticipation. When we finally did fall asleep, it was just before dawn, and we had reached that point where it was unclear, even in the gathering light, where she left off and I began.

While she made herself up to face the day, I pulled on my leathers and rode back to The Hospital, where I called Pinipaldi and left the message that I wanted to meet him for breakfast at a Mexican restaurant in one of Santa Barbara's numerous plazas. Then I called Isabelle.

She answered the phone on the third ring, and when I announced myself, her voice went cold as ice and right to business.

"Harry Hamilton called three times since you've been gone. He wants to meet with you and asked that you give me a progress report. Are you in the progress report business now? Also, Unity called and told me to tell you she has some information about coins for you."

"Anything else?"

"The leader of the elephant delegation called and said he had some new information for you—"

"I didn't expect to hear back from him so soon."

"Nestor, where were you last night? I called the house ten times and there was no answer."

"I went for a motorcycle ride."

"At midnight? At two in the morning? At four in the morning?"

Isabelle and I do not have the kind of relationship that encourages sleeping with other people. On the other hand, we don't have the kind of relationship which specifically prohibits it. What we have, however, is too good to ruin by lying. I lied anyway.

"I went up over the pass and stayed in Solvang overnight."

Solvang is one of the kitschiest towns in the known universe. It claims to be the Danish capital of America, and a lot of people of Scandinavian descent do live there, but really it's nothing more than a tourist trap with waffle restaurants, clog shops and a fake windmill.

"Solvang?"

"What is this, the inquisition? I took a ride over the pass and up the coast a bit. It got late and I stayed in a motel overnight. I just got home."

It was a simple, airtight, virtually unverifiable story.

"When are you coming home?" she asked.

"A few days. I'm out here for Harry Hamilton."

"So I shouldn't schedule any meetings until I hear from you? The Pakistani grocer sent a card. He wants to bring his family in to thank you personally."

"Hold off on meetings. If the lawyers call, you can fax me whatever documents you need to. Talk to the elephant people yourself and see if they've got anything real. Tell Unity I'll call her when I get back, and give me Hamilton's number. The grocer can wait."

In the years that I've known Isabelle, I've slept with two other women. The first was a one-night stand after an indiscreet overindulgence at a precinct barbecue in Queens. The other was one of the few women whom Amos Larsen has trained, a student perhaps overimpressed with my collection of black belts. Both liaisons were forgettable and short-lived, but somehow Isabelle ground them out of me in a foolishly romantic moment and has held them against me ever since.

The accusations hung in the air even after I hung up the phone. Some women have a way of making a man feel bad without saying a word, and Isabelle is one of them. I needed to stay busy to feel clean, so I went off to meet Pinipaldi and hoped to God that after a night with his girlfriend I could still look him in the eye.

I parked the Rolls in front of the place so I could keep an eye on it, and the hostess led me to the outdoor table where Pinipaldi sat waiting and sipping black coffee.

"Why coins?" he asked after I had ordered a croissant and herb tea.

"The foundation is heavily invested in real estate and securities. Tangibles interest me as an intelligent way to broaden the portfolio, particularly in the recession."

"What about your Japanese porcelain?" Pinipaldi countered.

I smiled. "You do your homework. Most of the porcelain no longer belongs to the foundation. It's been donated to a variety of museums around the country."

"We can make coins your business, too, Mr. Dark. I know just how to do it."

"I pay as much attention to making money as I pay to giving it away, Mr. Pinipaldi. I'm all ears. Sell me."

This made Pinipaldi smile and—gifted as he was at romancing the sale—he paused and ordered a glass of fresh-squeezed orange juice.

"A coin is a piece of art," he began, "but it's also a portable and enduring piece of history. If the coin is in a circulated grade—meaning that it has been out of the mint and used as currency—holding it in your hand as others have done hundreds, even thousands, of years ago can be especially satisfying."

"But not if it's in a plastic slab."

He winced. "Plastic slabs are primarily useful to the new collector or investor. Once you've found a reputable dealer, believe me, Mr. Dark, you have, you don't really need to buy slabbed coins."

Pinipaldi's innate sleaziness had been carefully nurtured and then sealed in by a thick layer of aromatic yellow wax. It was hard to see it through all that buildup, but I could tell it was there.

"What about counterfeits?"

He didn't bat an eye at the question.

"Not a problem," he answered smoothly. "Anything that's in a slab is guaranteed. Besides, there's very little counterfeiting going on anymore. Any reputable dealer will stand behind what he sells, slabbed or not. The real problem has been overgraded coins—specimens that a dealer claims to be finer than they really are—rather than fakes."

"Do fakes ever get slabbed?"

"I can't say that I've heard of that happening. The numismatists at the grading services are true experts."

"But somebody could make a fortune counterfeiting coins if he could get them slabbed. . . ."

"Really, Mr. Dark, counterfeiting isn't part of the coin scene anymore."

"So what can you do for me?"

"Act as your advisor and purchasing agent. As I told you yesterday at the gallery, people can make money in rare coins, but most people don't. That's because there's a tremendous amount of hype out there, a lot of misinformation, even a lot of *disinformation*. I can help you choose wisely, and find the coins you need, coins that represent limited downside risk, have true collector value and will increase steadily over time."

"Steadily or spectacularly?"

"I'm not in the hype business, Mr. Dark. If I told you that I routinely put together collections for my clients that increase at a rate of thirty percent a year, you'd go roaring off in your Rolls-Royce and stick me with the breakfast check."

"I'm going to stick you with the breakfast check anyway. Now tell me, what do you propose?"

"Charlotte and Dahlonega gold, specifically two-and-a-half-dollar quarter eagles. Those are time-honored collector pieces and in great and steady collector demand. Also early copper coins, which I believe to be highly undervalued at this time."

I reached for my checkbook and brought it to the table. He picked up his coffee cup in a rock-steady hand.

"One hundred thousand dollars." I ripped the

check off and handed it to him. "Don't spend it on counterfeits."

"I wouldn't know where to buy one," he said with a smile.

"You're too modest," I replied.

Chapter 19

HARRY HAMILTON CALLED The Hospital just after Morgan Pajaro agreed to have dinner with me that night.

"Whaddya got?" he asked.

"How'd you get this number?" I asked.

"You said you were going to Santa Barbara. I called information."

"I'm not listed."

"Your assistant told me how to reach you. Now what's the latest?"

I drew a deep breath at Isabelle's revenge and told him I'd met Pinipaldi.

"Is he our man?"

"Possibly. He's very smooth. I need more time."

"Every coin I buy makes me nervous these days," he said.

"Relax. I'll find your counterfeiter."

I pulled up in front of Morgan Pajaro's condominium five minutes early, hoping to catch her in some final state of undress, but when I rang the door she was ready to go, stunning in a white silk blouse, navy slacks and a quilted Oriental-style jacket.

It was a balmy night, and at Morgan's request I left the top down on the Rolls. We took the 101 freeway south along the Pacific coast, motoring in coddled comfort in Andrew Dark's Corniche, watching the headlights around us grow brighter as the dusk faded and the azure sky over the ocean turned deeper and deeper and finally to black.

At Oxnard we left the freeway and headed for the Pacific Coast Highway and Malibu. We followed the twists and turns of the road along the water, passing the Pacific Missile Test Center and the string of state beaches that led like tempting pearls toward Los Angeles. I had a Koko Taylor cassette in the stereo, but Morgan replaced it with Beethoven's Emperor Concerto.

"Beethoven always makes me think of the sea," she said, settling back into the rich red leather, her perfect white skin pressed against the headrest. "There so much bombast to him."

It was a pompous remark, but Morgan Pajaro seemed able to get away with anything. And besides, Beethoven is bombastic.

"Where are we going?"

"I'm taking a gamble," I replied.

"You took one when you invited me onto the back of your motorcycle."

"I mean about dinner. Do you like sushi?"

"So that's why the jacket's appropriate!"

"Well?"

"It's my favorite."

For half an hour, the notes of the Fifth Piano Concerto boomed around us, insulating us from the roar of the sea wind. At last Morgan broke the silence and the spell. "I come down this way a lot," she announced. She was gazing at the sea, and her words were faint.

"Michael has an estate in the canyon, on Mulholland Highway near Kanaan Dume Road."

"An estate," I repeated. "Must have sold a lot of coins to pay for an estate."

"Michael doesn't sell coins," she responded indignantly. "He creates investment portfolios for people, but the secret is that he ignores the trends and creates true numismatic collections. He probably knows more about United States gold and copper coins than anyone alive."

"You can't imagine how glad I am to hear that," I said, turning inland on Wilshire Boulevard.

I figured she'd find out about the hundred grand in due course.

There is an art gallery on Wilshire—located near a one-hour photo shop in a mini-mall—which masquerades as a Japanese restaurant. The owner-chef is an artist—and a businessman extraordinaire—from Tokyo. He disdains the taste of California fish and flies his "raw materials" in all the way from Japan twice a week. This makes for four-hundred-dollar dinners for two, but the eight-person sushi bar is always full because the food is exquisite enough to make an occasional flesh-eater out of even a die-hard vegetarian like me.

I pulled the Rolls up in front of the place and upped the top. Morgan Pajaro waited for me to open her door.

The restaurant was a temple to taste. Fish and other edible sea creatures were worshiped there, and the decor was elegant, but deliberately simple in order not to distract one from the masterpieces at the table. The other diners spoke in such muted tones that only the hissing of steamers and the occasional clink of kitchenware kept the restaurant from sounding like a church. We took off our shoes and added them to a small line of Ballys and high heels. Morgan looked impressed.

"A pleasure to see you again, Mr. Dark," said the maître d', bowing slightly. I returned the bow, and he led us to one of the restaurant's two private tatami rooms.

The tatami room is named for the bamboo mat that covers the floor. In the West it's not uncommon to find a pit underneath the low table, providing space for stiff legs. Not here. We had to fold ourselves under the serving area like pretzels.

We sat for a time, taking in the smells and sounds. When Isabelle and I are together, repartee abounds, but with Morgan I was quiet. Communication was proceeding nicely on other levels.

"Do we get menus?" she asked.

I shook my head. "Just wait."

We began with paper white slices of raw halibut topped with beluga caviar and presented on a shiso leaf.

"Doesn't even taste like fish," Morgan marveled.

"Not the fish we're used to anyway," I said, ordering a large bottle of sake. The rice wine arrived in a beautiful ceramic carafe with tiny matching cups, served to us by the soundless waiter. Morgan raised her cup.

"To coins," she said.

"For bringing us together," I responded.

Tiny pieces of abalone with Japanese string beans were next, followed by the skin of the hamo, an eel-like fish smoked and served with a tiny salad of vinegar-doused mixed vegetables. Morgan looked reluctant.

"Trust me," I said.

She took another swig of sake and popped the hamo into her mouth.

"It tastes like sesame seeds," she said with a smile of relief.

I stopped drinking sake as soon as I felt the familiar warmth suffuse me, but Morgan continued to drink all through the progression of raw fish that followed. Right after the Spanish mackerel, she put her toes below my lap and started rubbing.

"It's very sexy here," she said, her speech not quite slurred but certainly slowed. When the next dish came, she asked me to feed her. I picked up a piece of octopus in my chopsticks, but she shook her head, her dark hair following the motion a second later as if on some kind of video time delay.

"No chopsticks," she said. "I want to taste your fingers."

As I put the chopsticks down, she increased the pressure of her toes on my groin.

"Morgan," I began, shifting slightly and bringing one hand down to her bare toes.

"Your fingers," she commanded.

I leaned across the table and fed her the octopus with my thumb and forefinger. She took the fish in delicate bites, sliding her tongue over my digits with each nibble, chewing with her mouth only inches away from my hand, the heat of her breath reaching all the way to my wrist. When the octopus was gone, she sucked the sauce from my fingers, massaging me all the while with her foot, achieving the desired result.

The rest of the meal was delicious, but I hardly noticed. Morgan, however, insisted upon eating slowly and deliberately, taking occasional dishes from my fingers. When at last I physically removed her foot from between my legs, she announced that she was going to the ladies' room.

"Perhaps you'd like to join me?" she asked.

"I'll wait here," I answered.

"Your mistake," she said and left the room slightly unsteadily.

It took me less than two seconds to decipher the message, and then I got up and followed her. She didn't realize I was behind her, and when she closed the door to the toilet behind her, I was on it in an instant, pushing it open forcefully before she could shoot the bolt.

She gasped and turned around, but smiled when she saw it was me. I closed the door with my foot and crushed her to me, my hands busy at her pants. I had them open in a moment. She moaned and put her hands on the back of my head as I bent down.

I hefted her onto the sink, her thighs pressing hard against the porcelain. She bit my sport jacket in order not to scream, and we made love violently and passionately, the excitement of circumstances bringing us both to climax in moments.

I opened the door to the rest room cautiously and peered out, directly into the face of an actress I recognized.

"My mistake," I said quickly, and before she could

answer, Morgan locked the door behind me and I dashed into the men's room.

Back at the table, I asked for the check. The waiter brought it, and when Morgan returned we left quickly.

The actress was nowhere to be seen.

Chapter 20

THE NEXT MORNING, after another night of bliss with Morgan, I called the office and Isabelle promptly hung up the phone. I tried several more times and finally got the foundation's answering service. They indicated that Ms. Redfield had left for the day.

I tried Isabelle at the house in Redding and at her apartment. Finally I managed to get hold of Waku.

"You screwing up bad, Detective," he told me. "Isabelle will talk to you next year if you're lucky maybe sometime."

"Did she tell you why she's upset with me?"

"Hey, Detective, we're far away here, but we're not stupid people."

Hearing this, I headed for the Starship.

The airspace above most of the civilized world is crisscrossed with invisible paths. These "airways" are separate and distinct routes along which commercial, military and civilian aircraft must fly. Civilian airways are called Victors. I left Santa Barbara on Victor 183, heading sharply northeast over Bakersfield and Buttonwillow. From there I wanted to take a shortcut to Victor 244, the major coast-to-coast airway nearest to Santa Barbara. The shortcut required flying over Edwards Air Force Base and China Lake nuclear testing grounds. I called Edwards' approach to ask for permission to enter the Military Operations Area, but they were launching cruise missiles that day and told me to stay away. Hurry or no hurry, I wasn't going to get shot down, so I continued on Victor 183 to Porterville. When I reached the Fresno area, I got permission from air traffic control to jog east and join Victor 244 via Bishop and then Tonapah, Nevada.

It was a beautiful day for flying, and I was pushing the Starship hard, flying at thirty-five thousand feet and three hundred and thirty-five knots. The Beech chugs gas when you push it that way, but I figured I could afford it. Besides, ultra-advanced design or no, the Starship still had propellers and was no match for any jet Hamilton might be on. I needed to make time.

I tried to get Isabelle by phone all the way across Nevada, but there was no cellular network to pick up my call. As I crossed into Utah following the sun, I began to wonder where the hell all my good judgment had gone. Maybe Hamilton was after something he wasn't confessing, and maybe I shouldn't be so beguiled by a hot skirt.

A look at my charts and my fuel gauges told me I was going to have to refuel at Denver, so when I reached Hanksville, right in the middle of

Canyonlands National Park, I left Victor 244 for Victor 8, a northeast airway that leads straight to the Mile High City. Just as I crossed into Colorado airspace, I dropped down to three thousand feet to have a quick look at the Dark Ranch, climbing back up too quickly for all but the most anal air controller to object.

Even at twice their altitude, the Rockies were majestic before me, but when I began to overfly them, the air turned slightly choppy and they disappeared beneath a lumpy carpet of gray. I tried Isabelle again on the cellular phone, but I was still too far out of Denver to get a line. At Kremling, I called Denver's Stapleton tower.

"The peaks to the west of us are showing embedded thunderstorm activity," the controller told me. "Do you wish to divert?"

The view from the ground gives no hint of how badly a thunderstorm tortures the air. A really bad storm can rise eleven miles, a giant tube of wing-ripping winds and bolts of electricity, but a pilot can normally fly around the storm. I'd done it many times, and it's routine for a commercial pilot.

An embedded storm is something else: a series of storm "cells" surrounded by dark and dense clouds which make visual avoidance impossible and radar-assisted flying risky.

"How bad?" I asked Stapleton control.

"Commercial traffic is holding or going over the top. What's your ceiling?"

"Forty-one thousand."

"Not enough. We suggest you divert."

"Can you get me around it?"

"No guarantee."

"Have you been bringing private aircraft in?"

"Three, but conditions have gotten worse."

"I'm low on fuel. Give me a course."

The air traffic controller started my approach along Victor 8 with a steep eight-hundred-foot-per-minute descent. He was trying to bring me in right over the tops of the fourteen-thousand-foot peaks and below what he felt would be the worst of the storm.

Gaining airspeed, I dropped like a meteor toward Denver. As I closed in on the western peaks, the great wall that was the mountains melded with a dark gray wall of clouds. A moment later specks of rain dotted the cockpit glass and I was flying blind in a world of gray, the clouds close against my windows taking away all sensation of distance.

The Starship has among the most sophisticated instrumentation available to a private pilot, including a Collins dual-channel weather radar unit that tracks weather masses and detects turbulence. The stick thumping in my hands, I took my eyes off the clouds in front of me just long enough for a glance down at the screens.

At that moment the storm hit me. My stomach nearly came out my throat as a violent downdraft slammed the Starship toward the ground. The next moment I was pressed into the seat as a wind shear picked me up and nonchalantly threw me at the heavens as easily as a pitched penny.

The gauges were blurred and my hands were too unsteady on the controls to do anything more than hold on. I dared not throttle back for fear of jerking the lever too far and killing an engine, and the Starship's composite fuselage began groaning and crackling.

I needed to discover where I was, but I couldn't read my instruments and I couldn't see shit. I tried to radio Denver for help, but the plane was shaking so badly I couldn't get my finger on the transmit button. I looked up at the gray windows for a moment, and looked back down at the panel just as the cellular handset whizzed by my head.

I was flying upside down.

As I struggled to regain control, I cursed myself for making such a mistake in judgment and wondered what I had gotten into. The next moment two red lights flashed on, telling me that the engines were overheating. That meant I was climbing to a stall. Upside down. I looked at the altimeter, as the propellers desperately tried to bite air.

The Starship was burning its pistons trying to climb, and the storm was pushing it to the ground. For a brief moment I thought I felt a response to the stick, and grinned wildly thinking I had it all, but the next moment the inevitable happened. Inverted, and with no lift to keep the wings horizontal, the Starship stood vertical in the air for a moment until conflicting forces spun it like a child's top.

To survive the spin, I needed altitude. I had to go into a controlled dive so that the lift under the wings would allow me to regain control of the aircraft. But I had no idea how much room I had. A sudden downdraft could drop me ten thousand feet in a moment, and I didn't know whether I *had* ten thousand feet. Nonetheless, I had to risk it. I couldn't spin forever.

I throttled back as smoothly as I could and then pushed the stick forward. The plane suddenly pitched sideways as the instrument panel lit up with red lights. One engine was dead from fuel starvation.

I plummeted earthward under asymmetric thrust, one propeller pushing me sideways while the other feathered uselessly in the wind. Then, as suddenly as I had entered it, I was out of the storm. The air was calmer, and I could see. Above me, the bottom of the storm looked like the underside of a quilted mattress. The situation in front of me was not as good. There were mountain peaks everywhere.

My rudders were sluggish, and with one engine out, the Starship handled like a log in a swift-moving stream. I tried a restart, but one particularly high peak was approaching too fast and the engine wouldn't catch. I depressed the transmit button and told Stapleton air traffic control I was going down.

I banked as steeply as I dared to avoid the peak and squirted out across a small valley. There were trees everywhere, but no clearing.

Then I saw the thin black line of a country road. I headed for it, fighting to keep the nose up and the wings level, the storm above still causing fifty-mile-per-hour gusts as I neared the ground.

The average two-lane blacktop is sixty feet wide. The Starship's wings stretch fifty-four feet from tip to tip. It was going to be tight, but I was committed.

I set down, desperately steering with the nose wheel and the rudders when I touched, trying like a sports car driver to follow the curve of U.S. Route 34 as it headed for Longs Peak and Rocky Mountain

National Park. I managed pretty well, considering, until the utility pole took my left wing.

Then I plunged into a ditch and my head hit the instruments and everything went black.

Chapter 21

I WOKE UP with Waku's finger in my nose. Something in his expression stopped me from swatting it away.

"Your nose tube isn't straight, Detective," he explained apologetically. "I'm just straightening it."

"I told him he could," said a familiar voice.

Bewildered, I looked up to see Unity sitting on a chair near my bed.

"You're in the hospital," she said, rising and coming to me. "In Denver. You crashed your plane."

"Isabelle will be so happy," said Waku. "She hates that plane."

At that moment, the door opened and a tall man in a white coat walked in.

"Mr. Dark, I'm Dr. McPherson," he introduced himself. He was tall and sandy-haired, with a cauliflower ear and a veiny nose.

"You look like a McPherson," I said.

"As did my father and his father before him." The doctor smiled. "How are you feeling? Do you know where you are? Do you know what's happened to you?"

"How's my airplane?" I asked. Things were coming more and more into focus.

"Let's talk about *you* first. You have survived a plane crash. Remarkably well, I might add. You have quite a bit of bone bruising, but nothing internal and nothing that won't heal quickly with rest. You've also received a blow to your head. Again, nothing that we're terribly concerned about, but with any head injury, even when no organic damage appears, there is cause for caution. Do you know where you are?"

"Denver."

"Correct. Mercy Hospital."

"How long?"

"It's three-thirty in the afternoon. You crashed last night."

"Last night!"

"Just before dark. You were up near the town of Estes Park. You were brought here by a life-flight helicopter. Your office was notified, and your aunt and your, ah, chauffeur came at once."

I took some time to digest this information.

"Has anyone else come to see me?"

"Federal Aviation investigators have been most anxious to talk to you."

"That's all? No one else?"

"No."

McPherson pushed a button and the bed slowly raised me to a sitting position. "Would you touch the tip of your nose with your left forefinger, please?"

"What?"

"Just checking to make sure all your wiring's intact."

After watching me touch my nose and listening to me count backward for a quarter of an hour, McPherson agreed that my mental circuitry was in order and removed the tube from my nose.

"When can I leave for New York?" I asked.

"Your aunt warned me you might be like this." McPherson smiled faintly. "I'd like to keep you under observation for a while. You can't fly for a week or so anyway; the pressure changes are too dangerous after even a minor blow to the head."

"A week!"

"It's your brain, Mr. Dark."

"It's never been all that terrific," I said. "Maybe I'll risk it."

McPherson shook his head. "Let's see how you are tomorrow, but I'd put flying out of my mind if I were you."

As if on cue, the Feds came in. They told me that while I was unconscious, my insurance company had authorized that the wings be removed and the Starship towed to Stapleton, where it was awaiting repairs.

I gave them my best recollection of the crash, and as I talked, more and more holes in my memory filled up like empty drinking glasses under a fountain. They took notes, and told me that insofar as it was obvious that weather had been involved and another aircraft had not, and insofar as I had apparently followed the directions of an air controller, their inquiry was officially closed. They were very polite and told me that if I had any future questions, I should not hesitate to contact them. Assholes that they were, they wished me better luck in the future, commented that they were certain

I had an increased respect for thunderstorms deposited business cards on the table by the door and departed.

I took a nap for a time after they left, and when I awoke, Unity had pulled a chair up to my bed and was sitting and looking at me lovingly.

"How do you feel?"

"Like I just came out of the ring with Mike Tyson."

Unity smiled. "Poor Tyson."

"Does Isabelle know?"

She studied me for a long moment.

"We couldn't reach her last night. I tried myself several times. Waku went by her apartment, but there was nobody home. This morning, when we found out you were going to be all right, I called her at the foundation. The service said she was off working on a special project."

"I don't have her on any special project!"

Unity was silent. "I'm going to read your cards," she said at last.

"Would you excuse me while I call Isabelle first?"

"I just tried her again."

"I'm worried about her."

"I'm worried about *you*."

She took a purple cloth from her purse and unwrapped it to reveal the Tarot.

"A new deck," she said. "Chinese figures."

"What was wrong with the old one?"

"Nothing. I just felt like trying a new pack. Have a look."

She handed me the deck and I inspected it. It was a bit strange to see the traditional Tarot figures garbed in kimonos and robes, and I said so.

"It doesn't matter how they're dressed," she answered.

I shifted over and made a flat place on the bedclothes.

"Shuffle," Unity commanded.

I complied and handed the cards back to her. She lay four out on the bed.

"Only four?"

"It's called 'opening the key.' It's helpful for special problems."

"What special problems?"

Unity sighed.

"Oh, Nestor. You're in the hospital because you crashed your airplane, you don't know which coast to call home, the woman you love can't be found and you're doing something dangerous. Now let's listen to the cards."

They were the High Priestess, the Lovers, the Lightning-Struck Tower and the Fool.

"A moody or critical woman," Unity announced, fingering the Priestess. "Duality."

"Well," I said, settling back, my head beginning to throb.

She picked up the Lovers. "Decision time," she said.

"And the Tower?"

"A psychological crisis."

"I'm not sure I believe all this," I said. "Seems to me I'm just listening to an insightful friend."

Unity smiled and picked up the Fool. "You grow in humanity and wisdom," she said.

Just then the phone rang.

"Mr. Dark?"

"Last time I checked."

"I hope you're well, sir. This is Russ Tamarkin at Tamarkin Aviation out here at Stapleton field."

"Ah, my Starship."

"Yes, indeed."

"Well, how is it?"

"Mechanically it's in remarkably good shape. The nose gear is gone, as you might imagine. So is the left wingtip. The windshield needs to be replaced, and some sensors for the avionics are gone, but those things are plug-in."

"What about the fuselage?"

"That's the sixty-four-thousand-dollar question," he replied. "To be honest, we just don't have enough experience with the stress these composites can stand. We called Beech and they're sending somebody gratis. It's a new airplane, you know, and they're as interested as we are in how it stood up. It'll take a little time to evaluate things fully."

I thanked Tamarkin, hung up and fell asleep.

I didn't wake up until early the next morning.

"That's what I call sleeping," the nurse said admiringly as she brought me some orange juice and made little notes in her chart. "There's nothing like a bump on the head to quiet a restless soul, and word has it you *are* restless."

I asked her to find me Waku, but he heard his name and stepped in from right outside the door. Turned out he'd been there all night.

"Get all of us on the next flight to New York," I commanded.

"But the doctor said you could not fly."

"Just do it."

He smiled with delight. Waku loves it when I play king.

Chapter 22

MY PHYSICAL PRESENCE in New York did not produce Isabelle. Neither did driving to her home and mine. In frustration I called Bender from the back of the Benz.

"Where you been?" he asked me over the car's cellular phone.

"Doing research in California," I said.

"You sound guilty. What's her name?"

"Man, do *all* my friends have ESP?"

"Isabelle trouble?"

"You bet."

"You deserve it?"

"You bet."

"I'd invite you for a Carlsberg, but I've got this guy I'm supposed to see."

"I crashed the Starship."

"What?"

"Went down in a storm near Denver."

"Jesus, Nestor. Are you all right?"

"Could use a beer with a friend."

"I've put this guy off three times. You mind if he joins us? More I think about it, you *should* meet him, or he should meet you."

"So long as he doesn't need money."

"Now don't be nasty . . ."

"Bring him if you have to. I'll see you at the Brasserie in half an hour."

I circled back to the office and then to Isabelle's for one more look, so when I finally got to the restaurant, Bender was on his second Carlsberg. The young man with him was drinking Moussy—a French beer without alcohol. I was disgusted.

"Nestor Dark, I'd like you to meet Kevin Dilley," Bender introduced us.

Dilley, scrawny and in his late twenties, offered his bony white hand and rose to a full six and a half feet. He was scrawny and wore his clothes too big and his frizzy brown hair too long.

"I'm honored," he said.

"Don't be honored," I said. "But feel free to have a real drink."

"Nestor's a vegetarian martial artist who takes better care of his body than anyone I know," Bender interjected. "Don't let him intimidate you with any of his macho crap."

Dilley smiled. "I'm not a teetotaler, I just wanted to keep a clear head," he said. "This meeting is very important to me."

"I guess that's okay," I said slowly. "I eat sushi sometimes."

Bender explained that Dilley, along with an associate, ran a small, ultrahigh-tech company located in Soho.

"It's a robotics company," said Dilley.

"Kevin used to be a blues singer," Bender put in. "You two have quite a bit in common. He's got a very unorthodox background."

"I managed an apartment building, too," Dilley added.

The waiter came and I ordered two Carlsberg Elephants.

"Two Elephants, eh?" Bender said smugly. "I knew it was a woman." I ignored him and returned to the subject at hand.

"What you got going, Kevin?" I said.

"Kevin came to me for help in winning a NASA contract for his company," Bender answered for him.

"What's the name of your company, Kevin?" I asked, nearly grabbing the beer from the waiter's tray when it arrived.

"Moreman, Inc. We design robots for specialty purposes."

"And your exact position with the company?"

"He owns it." Bender smiled.

"What's the NASA project?" I asked, downing the last of the second Elephant and ordering two more.

"NASA is sending a probe to Mars," said Dilley, taking a swig of Moussy. "The mission will involve a surface landing. Once on the surface, the probe will disgorge a robot, which will retrieve samples from the surface, sort and evaluate them, then transmit pertinent data back to Earth."

"And you want to make the 'disgorgeable' robot," I guessed.

"We feel we are the best qualified," Dilley answered proudly. "We've had considerable success in prototyping other highly specialized models, for Pepsi, for instance, and for Disney Studios."

"Who else is in the hunt, and how long can you stay in business if you don't get the NASA job?"

Bender tapped Dilley's forearm. "I told you he was a quick study."

Dilley shifted uncomfortably.

"Don't bullshit me, Dilley," I said. "If I'm going to help you, I need to know the facts."

"It's a political problem, Nestor," Charlie Bender responded. "I know Kevin's work, I've seen his Mars proposal, and although I'm not supposed to admit it, I'm privy to the Grumman proposal, and to Lockheed's. Kevin deserves the work, but he has no credibility and no contacts. He works out of a warehouse in Soho above a doll factory, and his associates are foreign, young and iconoclastic."

"Iconoclastic," Dilley repeated ruefully.

"Grumman and Lockheed," I said. "Jesus."

I signaled for the waiter to bring me another pair of Elephants, and then looked long and hard at Charlie Bender. "You say he's smart?"

"Brilliant."

"Please." Dilley blushed, holding up his hands.

"You say he deserves the NASA contract?"

"I can't comment on the state of his business, but from the scientific standpoint, yes."

"Do you know much about the Dark Foundation, Kevin?" I asked Dilley.

"I know your reputation as a great philanthropist."

"Ah. Well, what you may not know, what in fact few people know, is that despite the size of our assets, we disburse only earnings. That means—"

Dilley interrupted me. "It means you only give away what you make. Is this a prelude to an offer?"

Bender started to drum the table nervously with his fingers as my fifth and sixth beers arrived.

"Other than the Mars probe, what projects are you aiming at?" I asked.

"We're developing the robot portion of a 'smart car.' "

I looked inquiringly at Bender.

"It's the transportation mode of the future," he explained. "It's already operating in Berlin. Infrared beacons read the location of a car and then guide it to its destination."

"How?" I asked.

"Well, right now the driver punches in his destination and a series of verbal commands tells him where to turn, how far to go, helps him avoid traffic jams, things like that."

"It sounds like Big Brother," I said.

"It's inefficient," Dilley expostulated.

I could see he was getting all worked up over the idea.

"People don't need or want that stuff if they're driving themselves," he continued. "They always figure they know better."

"I know I do," I said.

"Ah, but what if you're not driving! What if you're relaxing or reading or watching the television news while a robot responds to radio directions from a mainframe and whisks you through city traffic, around snarls and jams, avoids accidents completely and gets you to your destination faster than you could have driven yourself!"

"Not faster than *I* could have driven," I muttered into my beer.

"Nestor's an enthusiastic driver," Bender explained apologetically.

"Well, anyway, that's the beautiful part, the robot control mechanism," Dilley finished.

"There's a market for this?" I asked Bender.

"Ford's developing a version. So's Toyota and Fiat."

"Fiat?"

"They sell more cars than anybody in Europe," said Dilley.

"What's your plan?" I asked.

"Have it sooner and better than anyone else and sell it to the highest bidder," Dilley responded.

"And without the Mars project, what would it take to finance that?"

"Two-point-two million, and we keep control."

I smiled. "Of course. I'm not interested in control. I'm only interested in profit. I've got a foundation to run."

"I'm interested in control *and* profit," said Dilley with a smile. "I've got a company to run."

"I'll send two attorneys your way later in the week," I said. "We'll go through a due diligence. If your situation is as you've described it, maybe we can figure a way to get you your money in time to build beautiful toilets for visiting executives and buy Brooks Brothers suits for the artists among you. Perfect for landing that NASA contract."

Bender was beaming and Dilley was shocked at my decisiveness.

"And now, gentlemen, I've had a long day, and I've got a long drive home."

"You take Waku, we'll take a cab," said Bender as I stood to leave. I shook my head and he pushed a napkin my way. I took it, shook hands with Dilley and walked out of the Brasserie.

Out on the street I unfolded the napkin. Somehow unnoticed, Bender had scribbled me a note. It said he still wanted to hear about the girl.

Chapter 23

INSTEAD OF GOING home, I had Waku drop me at the office. Alone in the dark, I went to my secret toy room.

The room is dominated by my passion for target shooting. There is a shooting bench set up at one end, and targets on the opposing wall. Shooting inside a Fifth Avenue office building accurately and without damage requires special equipment. I use Olympic match air rifles, accurate to within a tenth of an inch at ten yards and capable of propelling a lead pellet at seven hundred feet per second, nearly as fast as the .22 Kimber.

But there's a lot more than a miniature shooting range here. Shelves of camera equipment line the walls, and remotely controlled cars, trucks, planes, trains and robots are lined up on the floor, each next to its own control transmitter.

I haven't always been a toy man. Before Uncle Andrew died, I was a rabid minimalist, a cop on the move with no appetite for goodies and no patience

131

for clutter. It always amused me that a man as wealthy and powerful as Andrew Dark could spend so much time flying eight-pound airplanes and rushing tiny dune buggies across the ruts and pits outside the Redding house.

But I learned to love them when I inherited them. I even installed a Murphy bed in the closet so that on days precisely like this one had been, I could yank on the rope and sleep with my toys.

Heavy with booze, I sat on the edge, too unsettled to go to sleep. I needed something hypnotizing to help me relax and put things in perspective. I needed to feel grounded to something—reassured by the familiar—and my Z-gauge train set was just the thing.

Some model-train enthusiasts decry Z gauge, irritated that it's so much more costly than the nearly as small N gauge, and is the exclusive domain of two German toy companies.

I'm an unpatriotic whore when it comes to toys. I don't care where the thing is made if it works well, and I'm not afraid of expensive electric trains. Z-gauge cars are the tiniest in the world, they feature workmanship beyond compare and price tags to match, and they work beautifully. Z cabooses have little gates on the back that open and close with a definitive click. The wheels on the locomotives are as finely polished and designed as if they were a critical valve on top of the oxygen sensors for the space shuttle.

I admire men who can make such toys. It takes a singular and complete obsession with detail, and the ability to utterly ignore the real world. There are times, when I am tortured by my own undisciplined philandering and made maudlin by too many Elephants, that I could sit and examine those tiny wheels for hours.

But wheel examining was not what I had in mind just then. Instead I moved the transformer controls over to the bed and turned the lights in the room down low, until I could just make out the glimmer of the engine and the parade of intricately crafted little cars behind it.

The toy room is too crowded to allow the re-creation of a Swiss lakeside or an Austrian village, even in tiny Z scale, so the track was set up around the perimeter of the room instead. Even at full zip, with the rheostat on the transformer turned all the way up, it took the tiny trains a few minutes to pass behind the air-gun targets, climb the ever-so-slight incline near the remote-control airplanes, complete the detour around the cocktail-serving robot and the wooden ship models and come clear around to the rifle racks and thence to the bench rests before finishing a circuit of the room.

That few minutes was easily long enough for the rhythmic buzzing and clicking of those tiny wheels to lull me to sleep—my feet where my head should have been—on the unmade Murphy bed.

Chapter 24

I AWOKE THE next morning fogged and in need of Unity's staunch and sensitive shoulder.

"You crash your plane, bash your head, fly and drink. Honestly, you're a child."

"I'm distressed you can tell I've been drinking."

"It's in your aura," she said impatiently.

"Silly of me." I smiled. "I should know I can't hide my aura from you."

"Don't you mock me, Nestor Dark. Especially since I've done you the favor of making an appointment with a coin expert I met through a Tarot client."

"Is he in Manhattan?"

"Of course, silly boy. How else would I have met him? I'm not a world traveler like you."

While Waku whisked us to the address on the piece of rose-scented paper Unity handed him, she quizzed me about Isabelle.

"She hasn't come to see you yet?"

"I haven't heard from her. I've tried everywhere."

Waku stopped the car in front of a distinguished-looking brownstone.

"She'll turn up," Unity said brightly.

Ronald Silver greeted us at the door. He was a gnomelike man about sixty years old with hair in an Einstein frizz. He wore a cardigan sweater and baggy gray wool trousers and carried a mahogany cane. Obviously delighted to see Unity, he ushered her in with his hand on the small of her back in a fashion that belied his age and completely ignored me.

"Come along, Nestor," Unity called. "Don't be shy."

The ground floor of Silver's brownstone was strewn with furniture which matched his cane: dark and heavy European pieces with claws for feet. The air smelled strongly of potatoes. Brass Tiffany lamps illuminated what would otherwise have been a dungeonesque living room. Finally acknowledging my existence, Silver gestured me to a wing armchair while he lowered himself onto the couch, shifting as close to Unity as possible.

"Ron, this is my nephew, Nestor," Unity said, winking at me.

"So you like coins," Silver said in a strong Yiddish accent.

"I'm interested in an investment-oriented portfolio," I said cautiously.

"Forget investment," Silver snorted, waving his old hands at me as if he were pushing away a plate of bad fish. "Enjoy the coins. Learn about them. The money will come."

"I'm interested in United States coinage," I said.

"Ron has quite a few American coins, as I understand," Unity interjected.

"Do you know U.S. gold?" I asked.

"Every serious numismatist knows the major pieces, but my love is copper."

"You mean pennies?" asked Unity.

Silver gave her an indulgent smile. " 'Cents,' not 'pennies.' Beautiful. Pennies are just the little things we use today. After the colonies joined together into a union, colonial coinage was replaced by federal coinage—that would be in 1793—and there were large cents and half cents, all fine designs struck in copper because it was soft and plentiful. Now they use zinc and just coat it a little bit. They make war machines and computers from copper."

Without our asking, he rose and hobbled out of the room.

"Be nice. Be patient. Maybe you'll learn something," Unity advised.

A few minutes later Silver returned bearing a shoebox. He placed it on the coffee table and withdrew a handful of large coins in plastic envelopes.

"You have to be careful about the kind of plastic you use," he explained. "Certain types will leave a dull residue on the surface of a coin."

He handed a coin to Unity, and I leaned forward for a look. It bore a woman's head on one side, her hair flowing back as if windblown, and a wreath on the other, encircling the words *one cent*.

"A 1793 wreath cent," he said.

"She looks like a witch," offered Unity.

"It's not in a plastic slab from a grading company," I observed.

That seemed to catch Silver's interest.

"Slabs," he snorted. "They're a boon to the lazy, that's all, and the investor segment of the coin market. There are really two distinct coin markets, you know. Collectors, and investors who speculate in the coins they think collectors will buy. People interested in early copper don't use slabs much. We like to clean our coins, and hold them and examine them closely."

"Cleaning doesn't ruin their value?" I asked.

"Not to the person who loves copper, and not if it's done properly, with compounds that do nothing but get some of the corrosion off without affecting the original surface of the coin in any way."

"It's interesting to think that somebody might have used this coin to buy something almost two hundred years ago," Unity murmured, turning the coin in her hand.

"That's the thing," Silver responded, obviously gratified that somebody understood what underlay his passion. "You need imagination to appreciate them, but you really are holding a piece of history. Ancient coins, two or three thousand years old, those are even more exciting."

"Does a coin like this appreciate in value?" I asked.

"I don't think that's the point, Nestor," said Unity.

Silver was plainly disgusted with me, and I was beginning to feel like a heathen, so I tried a different tack.

"What would your collection bring at auction?" I asked.

"All of it?"

"Yes."

"Two, maybe three million dollars, I suppose," Silver replied. "I haven't studied an auction catalog in some time, so I don't know the latest prices. I have some completely unique specimens."

His reply was so casual and unstudied that Unity dropped the coin on the floor.

"Don't worry," said Silver, scooping it up lovingly. "That's why we look at them over the carpet."

I knew that if I had dropped it, he would have pierced me from ear to ear with his cane.

"And you're not worried that any of them are counterfeits?" I asked.

Both Silver and Unity looked at me strangely.

"What are you asking me?" he queried. "I don't worry about counterfeits. I study my coins. These are my life. Nobody can fool me. Okay, one time I got fooled, but it's very difficult. Very, very difficult."

He wagged his finger at me. "Besides, you can't do it and make money. It takes too long, so much trouble. Such detail. A work of art."

"So if one wanted to make money counterfeiting, one would want to replicate only very valuable, investor-type coins."

Silver withered me with a look.

"Of course. But I told you, you can't make money with this. Unless you are a genius with your hands," he conceded.

"Nestor's a very successful businessman," said Unity.

"You said you've been fooled," I ventured.

Silver rose with the help of this cane and wandered the perimeter of his beautifully woven Persian rug.

"By Ozdal Bayirlar," he said with a rueful smile. "The man was a genius. He's dead now, but could he make copies! He did *everything*—Lydian, Lycian, Greek, Roman, Byzantine coins. All by hand with molds and rasps and soil."

"Soil?" echoed Unity, as fascinated as I was.

"With acid or base. To make the patina, so it looks really old, like it was in the ground forever."

"However did you meet him?" Unity inquired.

Silver's eyes got a faraway look. "That was in Istanbul. In jail, the poor man. After he fooled me and took my money. We had a laugh. I never liked a Turk except for him, even though he was a crook. He started out poor. He made coins for tourists, for people who wouldn't know the difference, who never even saw the real thing. He learned everything from his father, the whole family was crooks, he told me, but then he went beyond them. He discovered the money was in coins for *putzes* like me. He learned what we liked, and then he copied them."

"How did he get you?" I asked.

"With this one American coin. A New England Good Samaritan shilling." Silver shook his head and gave another rueful smile. "It was a joke. A famous counterfeit that he copied! It was 1862, you know, there were all these shillings around, like the Pine Tree shilling. But Ozdal was so good at copying the period; he had such an eye for detail. I thought it was real, a find, you know. And I paid for it. Oy, how I paid! I couldn't get my money back, of course; he was in jail, after all. When I saw his signature, I laughed so hard."

"His signature?" I said.

"Every counterfeiter puts some mark on his work," Silver explained. "It's part of their pride in their work. Could be their initials somewhere in a leaf or hair, or maybe a little sign that they always use. Like that. Ozdal's was in tiny *z* in one of the *o*'s around the coin's reverse."

"What did you do with the shilling?" I asked.

"Oh, I kept it. It was a brilliant work. He was a masterful craftsman, like I said. A genius." Silver plopped back down into his seat with a sigh. "But more important, there was so much to learn from him about coins. He was one of the most knowledgeable numismatists in the world."

He closed his eyes for a minute, and Unity looked at me and shrugged. We were sure he'd drifted off. Abruptly he snapped out of it.

"Thank you for reminding me of him," he said. "I enjoyed the memory."

Unity loves oysters, so I took her to the Oyster Bar in Grand Central Station for lunch.

"I never had an oyster until I met Andrew," she told me, dipping one lightly in horseradish and then slurping it up in expert fashion.

"I wonder why that doesn't surprise me."

"Does this interest in coins have something to do with counterfeiters? Are you working as a policeman again? Oh, do say yes—that would be marvelous for you, put the sparkle back in your eye. You were so happy as a policeman."

"I'm not on any police business, Unity. I'm just trying to help somebody out and learn something about coins."

"A counterfeiter?"

I had to laugh, and despite her look of obvious disgust, to order a Carlsberg.

"Really, Nestor," she said. "So many of those policemen were your very good friends."

"They still are," I said.

"A friendship doesn't last unless you work to keep it alive," she said.

My Carlsberg arrived, and I poured it long and slow, making a big head.

"Remember the weaver when I read your cards?" said Unity, choosing another oyster from her plate and using the tines of her tiny fork to break it free from its shell. "Attention to perfection in the creation of an object of beauty. Could that have to do with your counterfeiter?"

"I also remember obstacles," I reminded her.

"And love," she added.

As if on cue, Isabelle Redfield walked into the restaurant in the company of Harry Hamilton.

Chapter 25

UNCLE ANDREW'S MONEY allowed me so much mobility that everything, including a relationship, could quickly and easily become confining. Isabelle knew this, and she knew just how to play me. The moment our eyes met, she steered Hamilton to a distant corner of the restaurant. Unity was sympathetic when I lost my appetite and asked if we could leave, and we departed without so much as a glance in Isabelle's direction.

I had Waku drive me to Connecticut, something I rarely do. I was too deep in thought to trust myself behind the wheel.

"Has Tolstoy been eating his dry food?" I asked absently from the backseat of the Benz.

Waku nodded.

"And you've been combing him for fleas?"

"Women should bring home only vegetables," Waku observed as we cruised up the East River Drive.

"What?"

"Isabelle is like a woman who hunts meat, something a woman should never do. And you, you cannot decide to which tribe you belong. You have no tribe, Detective. That is your trouble. You have no tribe, and she hunts meat. And now there is another woman. This much I know."

I was in no mood for tribal aboriginal wisdom, so I raised the glass divider and sat in silence all the way to Redding. When we arrived, Waku opened the house for me.

"I could teach you a love magic song about the sea gull," he offered as Tolstoy bounded toward me baying happily, "but it's no use unless your heart is in it."

I didn't answer, so he roared off down the driveway, thrashing the Mercedes' suspension on the potholes. I went to the gun closet in the garage and withdrew a .22 Magnum Smith and Wesson 648 on loan from a friend.

I had used a .22 Magnum when I was a SWAT officer. Initially the other cops had ridiculed me for it, but they'd changed their tune after they saw that the little shell flew fast and true, and had a nasty propensity for following the canals of soft tissue, often traveling from arm to torso or leg to belly inside the body of the target.

Tolstoy followed me up the hill and I tacked up a target and let fly. The gun was built on the venerable Smith and Wesson "K" frame, and as such barely moved at all in my hand. The trigger was silky and the balance was fine, so I shot it until the barrel grew too hot to touch and the sky turned blue-gray the way it does on summer days before the sun bows out and I heard the sound of Isabelle's Mercedes.

I wandered out to the front of the house, wondering what I was going to say, but she got started before I had a chance. Even Tolstoy seemed to know better than to get close to her.

"The manager thing is about as far as it goes, isn't it," she half shouted as I approached. "I mean you like keeping me in a little box, each thing in a compartment, put away like the rest of your toys until you want raspberries and wine."

I figured that an offense was the best defense.

"Oh, come on," I snapped back. "I go off to California for a few days on business, you take up with Harry Hamilton—I don't think he owns another sport jacket, by the way—and you come up here to yell at *me*? Just like a woman."

She rushed me as if to sock me, and I drew back. I don't like it when people hit me, especially Isabelle, and she must have sensed my reflexes taking over.

"I didn't 'take up' with anybody, and don't you dare threaten me with your karate hands."

"Kung fu," I corrected, relaxing slightly. "My kung fu hands."

"Oh, who cares? It's just another one of your self-indulgent little habits, like taking off in your airplane whenever you want to."

I knew it was going to come back to my airplane. It always comes back to my airplane.

"That's the kind of guy I am," I said. "I fly my airplane pretty much when I want to."

"And what else do you do pretty much when you want to?" She had her hands on her hips.

"You look very sexy with your hands on your hips," I said.

It was a gamble, and it failed. I could see her color rising in the approaching dusk.

"You don't care much for responsibility, do you?" she rasped. "You expect me to hang around like *him*"—she gestured at Tolstoy with her foot—"while you disappear without warning, spend the night with whomever you please, reappear when you feel like it and expect things to be the same for us!"

I wanted to say I was sorry and to promise I'd change, but I couldn't. I wanted to offer her more of a commitment, but I didn't. Instead, her anger brought my anger, and the infamous Dark temper broke free.

"Don't you think you get paid enough?" I asked.

Even Tolstoy winced at that one. Isabelle stared at me for a long moment through squinty eyes, then backed away from me, got into her car and drove off.

I went inside to repack my bag for California.

Chapter 26

IT WAS NINE O'clock at night by the time I got hold of Waku and arranged for the charter of a Lear jet. Bender reached me on the car phone on my way to the airport.

"I'm off again," I told him.

"She must be good."

"Will you cut it out?" I exploded.

"Hey, take it easy. Have you got a few minutes to stop by the lab? I've got a new toy to show you."

"It's late, Charlie, and I don't like to fly tired."

"You won't be sorry!"

So I veered off onto the Cross County Parkway and headed down the west side of Manhattan until I reached the buildings of Columbia University.

Bender's lab was in a structure that looked like a cross between a museum and a morgue. There were sooty white Doric columns out front, and very few lights on in the building. I went in through a back entrance that is always open, but when I got closer to the inner sanctum—where top-secret defense contracts are pursued—I encountered locked doors and security guards.

One old-timer recognized me.

"Mr. Dark, right?"

"Right."

"Here to see Dr. Bender?"

"Right again."

"You know, I knew your father," he said.

"My uncle, actually."

"Ah, well, that explains it. You don't look a bit like him. I met him back when I was on the job, with the cops. He was rounder, if you know what I mean." He winked at me. He called Bender on the intercom and then buzzed me through.

Bender's desks are all specially constructed so that he can slide his wheelchair comfortably under them, and when I found him, he was poring over a small metal device that resembled the pin roller from a mechanical music box.

"Ha-ha, I just had to show you this," he said, handing me a little machine triumphantly. "Go ahead, guess."

"A brain for one of Dilley's robots?" I ventured, pulling up a chair beside him.

"Goddammit, Nestor, can't you think of anything but business? I told you this was a toy."

I shrugged. I wasn't in a playful mood.

"I'll give you a hint," he said, smiling. "You're going to try it out for me in Vegas, and it's going to make you money."

I stood up and backed away, shaking my head.

"Oh, no! Charlie! You're not back to that again."

Bender has, in the past, had a serious problem with gambling. A problem made worse by his association with my late uncle.

"No gambling! I promise! This is for you, for slot machines! Do you see any slot machines around here?"

I looked at him warily.

"I don't want any part of a gambling scheme," I said. "That thing must have taken months to put together. I know damn well you didn't make it for me."

"I did, I did," he insisted.

"And what am I supposed to do with it?"

"You're going back to California, aren't you? Make a little stop in Vegas. A little one. I just had to put the finishing touches on this when I heard you had business on the coast."

"No doubt it's illegal," I said.

He hesitated. "Well, I wouldn't go flashing it around."

"And you want me to bet a little of your green for you, am I right?"

Bender snatched the device from my hand, pushed his wheelchair back from the table and rolled over to what I took to be a large piece of testing equipment. It was shrouded beneath a sheet, and he pulled the sheet back with a grin and a flourish.

It was a slot machine.

Even knowing how serious Charlie's problem had been, I had trouble keeping a straight face.

"Where the hell did you get that?" I asked.

"What are you, my mother? Here, let me show you how it works."

"I think I know where you got that slot machine. Did you get it where I think you got it?"

"All right, all right, so Andrew got it for me in Atlantic City. That's no crime, is it? I mean, it's my money it pays me back with."

I couldn't help it. I started to laugh.

"Wait until you see it in action!" he cried.

He positioned himself in front of the machine and held the cheating device enclosed in his hand.

"These days every slot machine has a 'spin reels' button," he explained. "And that's made the machines easier for me to defeat. But you've got to *use the button*. Don't pull the lever!"

"All right," I said. "Then what?"

"It's a computerized magnet. There is a magnetic signature when the reels are lined up. Most machines pay on more than one alignment—four pears, for example, or three sevens—so there's no guarantee that you'll always win the big one, but you will always win."

"Charlie, Charlie, Charlie." I shook my head. "If it's money you need, why don't you partner with me in a technology company? I'll set it up for you."

"You're a good man, Nestor, even if your tastes are modest," he replied with a smile, "but I'm just trying to improve my odds."

"You won't try to sell this thing if it works?" I said cautiously.

"Certainly not! It's my baby!"

"You just want me to test it for you?"

"Just a little test."

"All right," I said. "A little test, but nothing more."

When I rose he asked to see my sport jacket and then made a big show of slipping something inside.

"Promise me you won't look until you're airborne," he said.

So I promised.

Then I drove to the terminal and got into my heavenly cocoon. I fired up the engines, checked all the instruments and headed for a night sky so twinkling and glowing it seemed full of coins.

Chapter 27

THE LEAR COULDN'T make it all the way to Santa Barbara, so I made a fuel stop in Lincoln, Nebraska, as close to the center of the country as one could ask for, and home of Duncan Aviation, executive airplane brokers extraordinaire. I had attended a number of airplane auctions held by Sotheby's at Duncan, and was always impressed by their service, the quality of their fuel and the winged beauties hangared there.

There was a stiff wind blowing when I set down in Lincoln, and the plane was unfamiliar. But with grim determination and more than a little bit of self-loathing, I managed a three-pointer. The air controller, watching me from the tower, offered a "Bravo" over the radio.

I was in the Midwest.

While the fuel truck filled me up, I stretched out in the hot wind of the plains, feeling the tension leaving my hamstrings and my neck. I made a quick walk around the airplane, took in the sights of an exotic jet or two nearby, slung my sport jacket over my shoulder and went into the terminal coffee shop.

I had the waitress bring me some hot water, and I opened two capsules of Siberian ginseng into it. I was sipping my tea when a man in an airport uniform came up to my table.

"Mind if I sit down?" he asked. "I'm 'Bravo,' just taking a break."

I gestured for him to sit, and the waitress immediately brought him a cup of black coffee.

"I'm always kind to a traffic controller," I said with a smile. "You never know when you might need one."

"That was some kind of landing. You fly fighters in 'Nam?"

"No, I just missed doing that. I learned on my own."

He nodded. "That's a pretty fancy airplane you got there," he said.

"Mine's a Starship. That's a rental."

"And what company you fly for?"

"A private foundation out of New York," I answered. "Philanthropists."

"And you're headed for Santa Barbara?"

It was cold in the terminal, and I shrugged on my sport jacket. When I did, I felt a weight in one pocket, and remembered Bender's parting gift. I took it out and put it on the table. It was a roll of quarters.

"Vegas," I said. "I'm going to stop in Vegas first. Do a little gambling."

"I guess they pay you well enough. Hey, listen, hope you don't mind me asking, but what in the hell is that you're drinking?"

So I explained the advantages of ginseng over caffeine, and discoursed on the virtues of the Siberian variety.

"Siberian ginseng goes down smoother," I said. "The stuff from China and Korea is a different plant, harder on the stomach. Either one's better than caffeine, though. Doesn't let you down so hard."

He stared at his brew.

"I hear that," he said. "I sure hear that."

So I gave him what I had left.

Unlike Lincoln, which shuts down about 10 P.M., the Vegas airport is an international field open all night to receive people from anywhere and everywhere, so long as they've got credit. The farther west I flew, the clearer the sky seemed to get, and when I dropped down into McCarran Field, the air was so clear the lights in the Nevada desert blinked like doll eyes.

A cab was idling in wait at the edge of the strip before the Lear's jets had stopped whining. Vegas is nothing if not a service town.

"Caesar's," I told the driver, fingering Charlie Bender's quarters in one hand and his slot-cheater in the other.

When I reached the reception desk at the great hotel and casino, I asked the clerk to ring the casino director, Mr. DeMeo.

"It's three o'clock in the morning," the clerk said pleasantly. "Mr. DeMeo would be in bed. Are you checking in? Is there some way I can help you?"

"You can ring Mr. DeMeo."

The clerk's eyes got a little harder. He was used to kissing ass, but he didn't like the look of mine.

"I'm entirely sure that I can take care of your needs, sir," he said firmly.

"Listen, if I tell Mr. DeMeo that you wouldn't wake him up, you'll be making your living recycling aluminum cans."

Without taking his eyes off me, he picked up the telephone.

"Security to the front," he said.

"Just tell Mr. DeMeo Nestor Dark is downstairs."

His mouth dropped open just as two husky guards with side arms and brown uniforms appeared as if from nowhere.

"Please escort Mr. Dark to the presidential suite, while I call Mr. DeMeo," the clerk said smoothly.

Paul DeMeo showed up at the door to the sumptuous five-room suite ten minutes later. His collar was undone, his eyes red-rimmed and his face swollen. Even so, he was the most debonair and dapper man of sixty imaginable, and he grinned with genuine pleasure at seeing me.

I felt like a spoiled kid for waking him.

"I loved the uncle, but the nephew's a pain in the ass," he said.

"Jesus, I'm sorry, Paul. I didn't mean for that jerk to get you out of bed," I protested, taking him by the elbow and sitting him on the perfect, soft leather couch. "I just wanted him to let you know I was here so you didn't think I was avoiding you."

"Your uncle Andrew used to do the same damn thing, popping in at strange hours unannounced. And he'd always ask for Irene. She's on her way over, incidentally."

"Paul, I can't see her. I'm involved with someone, and I haven't slept since yesterday. I'm exhausted."

"It's Sunday," he said. "Rest later."

"I'm pooped."

He shrugged. "You tell her. She'll be waiting by

the white tigers in ten minutes. You want casino credit?"

"I'm just going to play the slots," I said.

"The slots!"

"I've got too much of a reputation at the wheel," I said. "Your girls won't spin for me."

"Oh, yes, they will," he said. "And more."

I held up my hand. "I've got Irene to contend with."

"That's for sure. Now I'm going back to bed. Shall I see you for dinner tonight?"

"It's just a short visit," I said, patting him on the back as he walked to the door. "And thanks for getting up."

A few minutes later there was another knock on the door, and a bleary-eyed bellboy appeared with several new outfits, including a beautiful gray Armani suit and a stylish white shirt from Jekyll Hyde in New York.

"Compliments of the hotel, Mr. Dark, sir," he said, hanging them carefully in the closet. I slipped him a C-note and asked him to thank Mr. DeMeo personally. He was beaming when he left.

It was four o'clock in the morning when, clad in complimentary duds and smelling like a French whore, I made my way downstairs to the white tigers. Irene Park was waiting for me by the cages, a graceful, limber brunette who breathed animal sex and held her cigarette in a long silver holder.

Irene had been a teenage showgirl on the Strip when Andrew Dark had taken her under his wing more than a decade earlier. He had established a special relationship with her that went far beyond business, trying to interest her in school, even offering her a job. I've never understood why she refused, and my uncle's only explanation was that some people simply do what they have to do.

She watched my approach with a smile, and when I reached her, she kissed me lightly on the lips.

"You should have let me know you were coming," she said. "I might have been out of town."

"You're never out of town," I responded, linking my arm in hers.

"Shall we have a drink in the bedroom?" she said. "I assume you're in the presidential suite?"

"No fun and games tonight, Irene," I told her. "I'm just here to gamble."

"What's wrong with a lay before you play?" she asked. I winced. A thin wisp of blue smoke, driven by the currents of the casino's ventilation system, rose right into the nose of one of the white tigers. The cat raised a paw the size of my head to bat it away.

"You're the sexiest woman on earth," I replied, giving her a squeeze, "but I have some business here tonight."

"There's nothing like combining business with pleasure. I learned that from your uncle Andrew when I was only nineteen."

"My uncle was better at that than I am, but I'd like you to stay with me anyway. We're going to have more fun than you think."

So saying, I propelled her toward a bank of slot machines.

"Slots!" she exclaimed when I stopped in front of one and drew out Charlie Bender's quarters. "The Dark line is going to pot quicker than the eye can see!"

The casino wasn't very crowded, but I glanced

around anyway before withdrawing the cheater from my pocket.

"Watch," I said, dropping three quarters in and then positioning the machine over the reels the way Bender had shown me in the lab.

"Oh, my God, you're cheating!" Irene put her hand to her mouth.

"What does this machine pay?"

She glanced up. "A thousand," she answered.

"Good. I like to start small. Push the button."

She went for the handle, but I caught her arm.

"The button," I repeated.

The cheater worked virtually soundlessly, and completely without drama. All I felt was a slight warming in my hand and some static in the tiny tines. Then the gong went off, the lights started whirling and four thousand quarters began tumbling out of the machine, first tinkling into the metal tray and then spilling out onto the carpet.

By now, Irene was shaking her head and smiling. "You do appreciate the irony in this?" she said. "I mean, you could buy and sell this place and not even notice."

"I'd notice," I said, "but I do appreciate the irony. Anyway, you ain't seen nothin' yet!"

An attendant showed up to cash in the quarters, and while he was gone I moved over to a machine with four reels.

"Fifteen thousand," Irene breathed.

I dropped Bender's quarters in and nodded to Irene to push the button. She did, and I felt the warm static in my hand again as I held the cheater over the machine. Four pears lined up neatly and the gong went off, but the payout was only six hundred quarters.

"What happened?" she whispered.

"It just wins, it doesn't necessarily win big," I answered, scooping the change into several plastic buckets.

"You can't keep this up," said Irene, lighting another cigarette. "Somebody's going to notice."

As if on cue, the attendant returned with ten hundred-dollar bills. He smiled when he saw the buckets.

"Your lucky night," he said, disappearing with the loot once more.

"He doesn't know the half of it," said Irene, drawing closer to me as I walked to the progressive slots.

Every major casino has progressives. They are usually centrally located, often on a raised platform replete with neon signs flashing the ever-increasing jackpot. The lottery mentality at work, people watch the numbers climb well into six figures until some lucky winner goes home to a changed life and the neon returns to zero.

When we reached the podium, the jackpot was $314,766.

"Nestor, you can't," Irene breathed.

"I hate it when people say that," I said, and dropped five quarters—the maximum allowable bet—into the slot.

"Push the button," I commanded, holding Bender's cheater over the reels and disguising it in my palm from the eyes of a fat man in a paisley tie playing the adjacent machine.

When the reels stuck at four sevens, I felt like I was in the middle of a bombing raid. The lights flashed and the slot machine vibrated and the entire podium shook as people appeared as if from nowhere to crowd around their dream.

Security guards appeared, too, among them the two

who had escorted me to my suite. I nearly lost Irene in the flock of people milling after us as we made our way to the cashier. The guards formed a cordon around us, keeping the onlookers at a sufficient distance for me to hold the necessary conversation.

"Twelve equal checks," I directed the cashier. "All made out to Irene Park," I said. "Date them in consecutive months."

"That'll be twelve checks for twenty-six thousand, two hundred thirty dollars and fifty cents," said the cashier matter-of-factly.

Irene swayed like she was about to faint.

"What are you doing?" she managed, holding on to me for support.

"There are two conditions attached," I said, taking the checks and moving off toward the white tigers again as the guards dispersed the crowd. "First, you have to leave Vegas." I ticked off a finger as she watched my face. "Second, you have to get into another line of work." I ticked off another finger.

"Your uncle tried this," she said, her eyes filling with tears, the long line of her elegant and tired body quivering.

"That was then," I said gently. "This is now. You've survived this long. Quit while you're ahead. Take the first check and get out of town. Go wherever you want. Then call me in New York with your new address and you'll receive the other checks, once a month, until they're gone."

"I could lie," she said, looking me right in the eye.

"I know."

I kissed her gently on the cheek and headed for the presidential bed. When I got there, I made a single telephone call.

"Jesus, it's early there," said Bender when he answered the phone at his lab.

"It doesn't work," I said. "The damn thing doesn't work at all."

Then I hung up.

Chapter 28

I CALLED MORGAN the minute I got back to The Hospital.

"You back in town?" she asked.

"I just flew in. I haven't slept all night."

"Should you fly when you're tired like that?"

"No, I shouldn't, and to make up for it, I'm sitting in a big black Jacuzzi and the water is swirling around me and I'm wishing you were here. Will you have brunch with me, or does Michael have you busy?"

"He's out of town, and I was just going to spend some time working at the gallery."

"Come to my place instead. You won't be sorry."

I got out of the tub and drove the Corniche down to a local health-food restaurant for some healthy takeout. When I returned, I found Morgan sunbathing topless in my favorite deck chair, a Walkman on the ground beside her, headphones in her ears and tanning goggles over her eyes. She was moving ever so subtly to the music, and her heavy breasts swayed to the beat. I stood with the food before me and stared until what Unity would have called my "male aura" woke her up and she reached for the tape machine.

"You look awful," she observed.

"Lack of sleep."

"I hope you don't mind that I let myself in. The back door was unlocked. Your house is beautiful. I love the way it's so clean and spare and empty. It makes me feel peaceful."

"I wish I could take credit for it," I said, setting down the food. "But my uncle Andrew did the decorating, or had it done."

I bent down and put one of her nipples in my mouth. The sun had made her sweat just a little, and the scent was exhilarating.

"Tell me about him," she said, gently pushing me away. "He seems to have had quite an effect on you."

"What do you want to know?"

"Was he like you?"

The question surprised me. The people who know that I am Andrew Dark's nephew generally knew him and are therefore more interested in whether *I* am like *him* rather than the other way around.

"No," I said slowly, "at least not much."

"But you like the things he liked. I mean you could have redecorated the house, but you chose not to. You drive his car, too, don't you? You could have bought a Ferrari or something."

"I always figure he knew better," I replied. "He was older, he always had money, he had time to develop taste and class."

"I've always thought a person was born with taste and class," Morgan said, rising from the chair in a smooth yet wobbling motion that nearly stopped my heart and making her way to the food.

"Some people are. I don't think I was."

"Maybe you're wrong. Maybe keeping his things because they're beautiful is the tasteful and classy thing to do."

"I think it's because I'm a coward, but thanks for the vote of confidence. May I eat some of that broccoli pâté off your breasts?"

"No, you may not. At least not until you've shown me the rest of the house."

"Let's begin in the bedroom," I said.

"I'd prefer the basement."

So I showed her the garage. She ran her hand over the Guzzi and barely brushed the cold, smooth paint of the Corniche with her half-bare buttocks.

"What's that in the corner?" she asked, pointing at the universal set.

"Weights."

"I know weights when I see them, Mr. Dark. I'm talking about the wooden thing."

"It's called a wooden dummy. It's for exercise."

"Your martial arts?"

"How come you know so much?"

"Why shouldn't I?"

Fatigue more than modesty stopped me from offering an exhibition, but she demanded one anyway, so I positioned myself between the protruding oaken arms and began to move.

Morgan stood over to one side of the dummy. The sight of her next to the wooden pole was distracting, to say the least, but I persevered, swatting one wooden arm and then the next, cupping here with a crooked hand, kicking there with the edge of my heel. I became so entranced that I didn't notice what she was doing until she moaned.

"Jacuzzi," she said breathlessly, taking her hand away.

I may be serious about my Wing Chun, but I'm no fool. I took her hand and led her upstairs to the swirling black waters.

Later, after the bath was over, Morgan put on my navy blue terry-cloth robe and we dipped into the food on the terrace.

"Michael told me about the money you gave him," she said, taking a minute quantity of pâté on the end of a piece of celery.

"And?"

"I approve, of course. He's a brilliant numismatist and a brilliant investor. You won't be sorry."

"Do you do any of the investing?" I asked.

"I do all the research. And I handle important clients."

"To coin a phrase," I said.

"Very amusing."

"So you don't actually put portfolios together."

"Michael doesn't feel I know the markets well enough for that."

"I worry about counterfeiters," I said suddenly.

She started, and my uncle's monogrammed drinking glass went crashing to the floor. It shattered.

"I'm so sorry," she said, bending hastily to pick up the shards.

"Watch you don't cut yourself," I warned, feeling suddenly and terribly sad as I picked up the shard with "AD" inscribed upon it. I went to the kitchen and returned with a whisk broom and a dustpan.

"You don't have to worry about counterfeits as long as you buy from Michael," she said conversationally as I swept. "He's too honest and knowledgeable to let a counterfeit slip by. That glass was your uncle's, wasn't it?"

"Yes."

"You never did tell me anything about him."

"I told you he was a man of taste and class."

"Was he ever married?"

"He had a girlfriend."

"Here?"

"In New York. He didn't spend much more time in Santa Barbara than I do."

"Maybe you'll spend more."

"Maybe I will."

"What did he look like?"

"Elegant."

"Did he fly his own plane, too?"

"He was afraid of planes. He wasn't very physical."

"I like that you're physical. Would you take me on another motorcycle ride?"

"All right."

"Now?"

"Now?"

"I want to ride by the ocean."

"Your wish," I said with a sigh, "is my command."

Chapter 29

DESPITE MY CALLS for safety, Morgan insisted upon motorcycling south from Santa Barbara wearing only a bikini. The scenery by the sea was fine, but the air was cooler than it had been in Santa Barbara, and by the time we reached Point Hueneme, her skin was a mass of goose bumps, and she nudged me to stop the bike.

I pulled over north of Zuma Beach and offered her my jacket.

"I need more than this," she said, shrugging on the deerskin.

"I'm not going to say I told you so, but I don't know what we can do."

"I have to get some clothes on or I'll die of hypothermia," she said.

"You won't die, but you will catch cold."

"I have some stuff at Michael's ranch; it's just down the road from here."

I gave her a long look searching for a setup, but there was nothing in her expression but chilled.

So she directed me into the L.A. canyonlands, and I followed her gestures through the twists and turns away from the sea, wondering all the time why she was with me, what Pinipaldi was planning, why I believed Hamilton that there even *was* a counterfeiter, what he was doing with my girl and how I was going to get Isabelle to forgive me if I kept riding around with a half-naked woman who made my blood boil.

Pinipaldi's ranch was situated on a wild stretch, higher than the Hollywood Hills, which support Mulholland Drive and more rural than anything short of the deep desert of Lancaster and Palmdale, where people race cars on dried-up lakes and the government hides missiles deep under the sagebrush.

The estate was surrounded by a low, white metal fence, which Morgan informed me carried electronic information to a nerve center in the garage. Pinipaldi, she told me, would know if a ground squirrel farted within a quarter mile of the house.

"Why all the security?" I asked.

"Michael doesn't like to be disturbed," she told me as she put a funny-looking round key in the hole of the metal arm that rose to meet us at the gate and then punched seven numbers into the keypad. The gate slid silently back to admit us.

"Does he conduct business here?" I pressed.

"This is kind of his retreat. He calls clients, checks his books, puts deals together, does research."

The driveway reminded me of a paved version of the one that led to the Redding house, but the dry Pacific soil supported only gums and palms. The house itself was low and square, sprawling awkwardly over the land like only a homestead west of the Rockies can. The inside was built luxuriously around an indoor-outdoor Japanese garden with a Jacuzzi in the middle.

"Michael sometimes sits in there for hours," she said, putting down her things and gazing at the plethora of perfectly nurtured bonsai trees growing out of carved and artfully arranged rocks and ledges and paths. "He did the whole thing himself. Now, if you don't mind, I'm going to jump in that hot tub before I grow icicles."

"I'll have to look around," I said.

She looked surprised that I didn't want to join her.

At the end of the front hallway, in the westernmost corner, there was an all-glass observation room built a half-flight up from the rest of the house. The room afforded a fantastic view of the ocean, yet hugged the hillside closely enough to be virtually invisible from the beach. It was a view to match the one from the Dark villa in the south of France, but I kept that observation to myself.

There were several other bedrooms, a library studded with coin books and an exercise room. There was also a locked door near the observatory, and I returned to the garden and asked Morgan about it.

"Private storage, I think," she said, floating gloriously naked in the tub, her eyes closed, her face relaxed.

"You feel better?"

"Heavenly."

"Shall I light a fire?"

"It's summer." She laughed, her eyes still closed.

"It's cold and you're freezing. Let me light one."

So I did, and we sat together on pillows and warmed ourselves and made languorous love.

I awoke to find the room lit by moonlight and

Morgan deep-breathing beside me, her eyes fluttering with a dream. I watched her for a few minutes to make sure she didn't stir, and then I went for the storage room.

The lock fell quickly prey to the small set of lock picks I carried in the change pouch of my wallet, and I opened the door to reveal row after row of glass cases filled with coins. It seemed an oddly insecure way to display valuables, and I turned on the overhead light for a closer look.

It was a collection of counterfeits.

A carefully typed index card was affixed to the case beneath each coin. The cards contained biographical information about the forger or indicated that he was unknown. Also present were identifying characteristics of the coin, as well as numismatic data on the genuine coin and the date that the fake was acquired by Pinipaldi. The collection was extensive, and according to the cards, my tasteful friend had been interested in duds for some time.

I was thinking about the size of Pinipaldi's balls when Morgan walked in.

We stood looking at each other.

"I don't like this at all," she said.

"Yeah, well, I don't like it either. These are all fakes."

"Michael collects them," she said, cinching her bathrobe tighter.

"Why didn't you tell me?"

"That Michael has a collection of counterfeits? Lots of dealers have them. Apparently they're quite fascinating."

"You told me you didn't know what was in here."

"Look, I figured if he wanted to show you sometime, he would. I brought you here as my guest. I didn't want to betray Michael's trust."

"There's a laugh," I said.

The Dark mouth got me a cold night alone on the couch.

Chapter 30

MORGAN LET ME grudgingly back into her arms just
before daylight, and for hours we made the kind of
love that makes for weak knees and heavy bones.
When she realized the time, she had me take her directly to the gallery in Montecito.

If I had been any less of a gentleman and not escorted her all the way down the ivy-draped walkway
to the door of Tangible Scarcities, I would not have
seen Michael Pinipaldi put his hand on Harry Hamilton's broad back and usher him quietly into the
gallery.

I froze with my hand on Morgan's arm.

"What is it?" she asked, annoyed and shaking free.

"Someone I didn't expect to see here."

"I have to go to work, Nestor. I don't have time
for cat-and-mouse."

I peered around the door as she opened it, but
Pinipaldi and Hamilton were nowhere to be seen.

"They're in Michael's office," she said softly.

I reached over and turned on the intercom on her phone.

"Drink?" I heard Pinipaldi ask.

"Beer, if you've got one," Hamilton answered.

"I think I can round one up for so persistent a businessman."

"What do you know about the Wall Street coin funds?"

"Every coin dealer's heard of it."

"I run one of the original ones, maybe the biggest. I do all the buying. I started the fund, Mr. Pinipaldi, and its performance is the basis of both my continued employment and my future fortune. Are you receiving me?"

"You haven't said anything yet," said Pinipaldi.

"In order for the fund to do well, I need to buy low and sell high."

"How many coins are we talking about?"

"It's not so much the number," said Hamilton, "it's the type. You see, I know about you."

"Who is this guy?" asked Morgan.

I put my finger to my lips.

"I beg your pardon?" Pinipaldi answered.

"I happen to know that you are the source of some very, shall we say, 'unusual' coins."

"I do have access to fine material," Pinipaldi agreed, "and I'd be happy to help you put together some pieces which I think would stand your fund in very good stead."

"You can't buy the kind of coins I want," Hamilton said. "You have to make 'em."

"Kindly get to the point," said Pinipaldi.

"My sources tell me there's going to be a run on

early copper at the end of the summer," Hamilton continued. "It wouldn't be a bad thing if you could make me a handful of draped-bust large cents, a 1799 maybe. I can drive the prices up and we'll all be happy, and your side will be risk-free."

"Oh, my God." Morgan whispered, covering her mouth.

"Get out of my gallery!" Pinipaldi stormed.

I put my hand on Morgan's shoulder, preparing to move her out in a hurry.

"This is purely a business proposition," Hamilton countered. "No one will ever know."

"I said *GET OUT!*" Pinipaldi roared.

Afraid Pinipaldi would hear the echo of his own voice, I jumped to tap off the speaker just as I heard the familiar sound of knuckles on jawbone and a crashing thud.

"Maybe you're the man and maybe you're not," I heard Hamilton say. "But if you ever repeat this conversation, you're dead. Believe it. I'll kill you myself."

Morgan went for the door to Pinipaldi's office and I intercepted her, put my hand over her mouth and moved her, ducking and resisting, out the front door and behind an ivy-covered colonnade. A moment later Hamilton burst through the front door, looked around quickly and jogged off toward the parking lot.

I took my hand from Morgan's mouth.

"Don't ever do that to me again," she said.

"I'm sorry. I didn't want you to confront that man. He's dangerous."

"You *know* him?"

"I thought I did, but I was wrong."

We went back inside and I checked Pinipaldi's

carotid. His breathing was regular and his lids were starting to flutter.

"He'll be all right," I reassured Morgan, and slipped out before Pinipaldi's eyes started working and he saw what was really going on.

Chapter 31

Too TIRED TO fly myself, I hired a limo to take me to Los Angeles and took the red-eye to Kennedy. I tried Isabelle from my first-class seat, but all I got was her recorder at home and the service at the office. It made me feel silly for not having more staff, and I resolved that whatever else came out of the events of the past week, I would have to hire another assistant. Leaving a third-of-a-billion-dollar philanthropic foundation untended because of one woman's temper was patently absurd.

I tried Morgan, too, but she was furious at me for skipping town after what had happened to Pinipaldi. She said she was upset. I said I was, too. All I knew for certain was that things were very much out of control. I had many more questions than answers. It was clear that Hamilton had duped me. I had no idea where I stood with Morgan and no idea whether Pinipaldi was the man I sought. I like to be in control and I wasn't. It was not a good flight.

Waku met me at the airport and took me straight to the office. I was hoping to find Isabelle there, but the place was empty. I tried Hamilton, but all I got was his secretary.

"I'm sorry, Mr. Dark, Mr. Hamilton's still not in the office. Are you sure I can't connect you to Mr. Tibbet?"

"Do it," I said.

Tibbet came on the line, obviously wowed by the reputation of Andrew Dark. His speech was obnoxiously punctuated by "yessirs," and "if-there's-anything-that-I-can-do-sirs."

"Is Mr. Hamilton on vacation?" I asked.

Tibbet's pause told me tomes.

"He does still work for the firm?"

"Oh, yes, sir, Mr. Dark, absolutely, sir. He just took a couple of days off to attend to some personal business. Are you interested in the coin fund, Mr. Dark? I'd be happy to come and meet with you and tell you all about what we're doing. I'm sure you've heard of our success. We're very excited."

"I'd prefer to speak to Mr. Hamilton directly. Would you locate him for me, please?"

"We'll certainly do our best to have him get in touch with you right away, Mr. Dark. And like I say, if he doesn't call you by early afternoon, I certainly will. There's a very exciting future for you in numismatic investments, Mr. Dark."

The moment I hung up with Tibbet, Isabelle Redfield came walking back into my life. She looked smooth and perfectly pressed and she smelled of Bal à Versailles.

"Where the hell have you been?" I demanded from behind my desk.

"Where the hell have *you* been! Some guy named

Kevin Dilley has been calling here every few hours about some robotics company."

"Moreman, Inc. He's waiting for the lawyers."

"Yeah, well, thanks for letting me know."

"Well, thanks for rushing to my bedside after I crashed my plane."

"Well, thanks for letting me know you were out of town again. They fix your airplane that fast?"

"I rented one. And I'm fine, thanks for asking. Now you want to tell me where you've been?"

"Not particularly."

"With Harry Hamilton?"

"Listen, Nestor," said Isabelle. "You have made it perfectly clear that you are not accountable to me for your actions. I am therefore not accountable to you for mine."

"What are you talking about? I take a trip to California, a business trip, I might add, and I spend the night up the coast on my motorcycle and you go batshit!"

"Batshit?" Isabelle asked deliberately. "Your little bird called here day before yesterday. She wanted to know if I knew where you were. She said you two had a date in Santa Barbara but you hadn't shown up. She was just wondering if urgent business had called you away. I told her I was sure it had."

"What little bird? What are you talking about?"

"Morgan Pajaro. 'Pajaro' means 'bird' in Spanish, Mr. World Traveler."

"It's not what you think," I began.

"Oh, it's exactly what I think," said Isabelle. "And that's just fine. I've been playing this game by your rules for too long anyway. Now I'm going to set some of my own."

She tossed her gorgeous mane, sat down and produced a notepad.

"The elephant delegation called," she read, avoiding my eyes. "They're anxious to see you as soon as possible. We've also received two new business proposals which I think you should review. One has to do with plastic houses, the other with organoids."

"Harry Hamilton's a crook. I'm going to take him down. Now will you tell me where you've been? Have you been with him?"

"Take him down? All this money and all your traveling and you still talk like a cop. You're boring, you know that? When you started the foundation you were an interesting man, full of excitement and enthusiasm over doing good in the world. Then you got cynical and self-involved. And spoiled."

"I know," I said quietly. "That's why I'm doing what I'm doing."

She looked floored.

"And what is that?"

"I told you on the phone from California, I'm investigating again. It's good for me. I need it. I've forgotten how to act."

"I'll say."

"You just did."

"Right. Now, I gather that you know what an organoid is?"

"An organ whose pants are too short."

"I see. And do you know as much about plastic houses?"

"A place for plastics to go when they're old and tired?"

"There are times," Isabelle pronounced in precise

and measured tones, "when it's hard to believe that you are an adult."

"All right." I sighed. "Tell me about organoids and plastic houses."

"Plastic houses are the wave of the future. In fifty years they'll be made in factories by robots and they'll cost one-quarter the price of a regular house."

"Plastic's a petroleum product. It doesn't sound good for the environment. What about organoids?"

"The latest biotechnology. You take a cell from a person's liver, say, and you culture it to grow a new liver. All the genetic information's there. The idea comes from salamanders. They grow new toes or tails if they lose them."

"Is this for transplantation?"

"Nope. In a way it's easier, because there's no tissue rejection. They take some of the healthy cells out of a diseased organ and *then* culture a new liver from it. All in the same person; no other donor involved."

"I'll want to get Dr. Bender's opinion on it."

"I've already sent him the information with a note from you asking for his comments."

"Thank you."

"Won't you consider the plastic houses?"

"Sounds like a good business, but not the kind I want to be in."

"When should I schedule the elephant people?"

"Have them send their proposal in writing. If I like it, I'll see them again."

She made a couple of notes on her pad.

"Anything else?"

"Tell me everything you know about Harry Hamilton."

Isabelle turned on her heel and left my chambers. It was obviously time to kill some paper.

I went to the toy room and surveyed my collection of air pistols. My favorites were a Pardini Fiocchi K-58 single-stroke pneumatic and a Feinwerkbau Model 65 Mk II. Both were deadly accurate pieces, capable of grouping five .177-caliber pellets within a circle one-tenth of an inch in diameter at thirty feet. The German gun was beautifully designed, cocking with the single stroke of a lever on the side of its barrel. Although cruder in fit and finish, the Italian gun was more svelte in outline, and its superb wooden grips made it feel more sensual in the hand. After the brush-off I had just received from Isabelle, I needed something that felt good in my hand. I took the Pardini.

I put a fresh target up and returned to the bench. I stood in competition stance with my right hand outstretched and my left behind my back. I lined the sights up with the central black dot at the end of the range and began the slow squeeze to power when suddenly the black dot spread out wider and wider until it covered my field of vision and I felt like I was in Denver again.

This time when I woke up, Isabelle was crouched next to me, her cool hand on my brow, her eyes close to mine.

"Are you all right?"

"I guess I should have listened to the doctor."

"Do you want me to call an ambulance?"

"Forget that." I looked around the toy room for a moment, then struggled to my feet, still feeling light-headed.

"Well, then, perhaps you're well enough to take a *very important* call from Miss Pajaro. She sounds *very, very* upset."

"You know you're acting like a child," I said, following her woozily out to the phone.

"Takes one to know one," she said.

"Ah, now that's much more mature."

I took Morgan's call in my office, but when I picked up the receiver there was nobody there. As I hung up, the other line rang, and I answered it myself.

"The Dark Foundation," I said.

"Nestor?"

The voice was almost unrecognizable through the sobs. The woman was hysterical.

"Morgan? I just picked up the other line. . . ."

"I couldn't hold. Nestor. It's Michael. He's dead."

Chapter 32

THE SLUG THAT removed the right side of Michael Pinipaldi's face proceeded through his brain and vaporized the display case where gold coins had once slept in velvet. It was, according to the ballistics report from the Santa Barbara PD, a .357 Magnum probably delivered by a silenced revolver, which would explain why nobody heard the shot and why Morgan Pajaro was unfortunate enough to discover the body all by herself, early the next morning, when she arrived for work at the gallery.

Procuring this information was no easy task. My contacts with the Santa Barbara heat were essentially nil, forcing me to rely on my tempestuous relationship with my former commanding officer, Giuseppe Rignola. When I inherited the Dark fortune and quit, Captain Rignola went through a few months of refusing my calls, still bristling because I added the insult of taking Waku as my driver to the injury of depriving him of his best trigger man. After that came a half year or so during which he dwelled constantly on the fact that I carried more in my wallet every day than he had in his entire pension plan. Things finally got better when he started reading about the foundation in the newspaper and realized, as a result of what I had to agree was a bizarre perversion of fate, that I would probably be a good friend to have.

Knowing that didn't improve his manner any.

"Better not be asking me for any more favors," he told me, reaching across his desk and snatching back the fax sheet. "You're lucky I persuaded the SBPD not to haul you in for questioning. You're one of the last appointments recorded in his book."

I threw up my hands.

"I owe you," I said.

"More than you think. You know something, Dark? Your uncle's clout put you on such a fast track to SWAT, you never really learned much about street folk."

"My uncle's money?" I questioned him.

"Tell me that surprises you and I'll show you a guy who really believes that the whole world is what you see through a seven-inch sniperscope!"

"I was damn good at what I did, never mind my uncle!"

"At shooting? Yeah. You were the best. At street smarts? I'd say you have a thing or two to learn. Now what the hell do you have to do with this murder in Santa Barbara? And give it to me straight, Dark, or I'll hand you to the Feds in an eyeblink, foundation or no foundation."

"I'm dating the girl who works for the deceased," I said.

He looked at me suspiciously.

"In Santa Barbara?"

I nodded.

"Isabelle know about that?"

"Oh, sure," I said. "I give her the blow-by-blow every night."

"Just proves true what I always say. Money don't make you any smarter, it just makes you richer."

"I'm thinking about maybe not seeing her anymore."

"Good move." He nodded approvingly. "Now you want to tell me why you were in Pinipaldi's appointment book if you were dating his girlfriend?"

"She told me that coins might be a good investment for the foundation, convinced me to talk to him."

At first I pretended I didn't know why I was lying to Rignola, but when I left his office, I confronted the fact that I wasn't *protecting* Hamilton, I was saving him for myself.

Like hiding the last piece of plum pudding and hard sauce, like salting away the last little bit of milkshake. Hamilton was someone I wanted to devour. He had lied to me and used me, murdered a man based on information I had given him, and last but not least, he had bedded my girl.

I had a thirst for Hamilton's blood that just wouldn't quit.

I had two stops to make with what was left of the day. The first was at Ron Silver's apartment. Waku remembered the address, and he whisked me there in the Mercedes while I desperately flipped through three new books on coins.

I ran up the steps of the brownstone and pressed the buzzer. Waku could have given the Benz a valve job in the time it took Silver to get to the intercom, and when he did, he didn't sound pleased that it was me.

"Your auntie with you?" he rasped over the speaker.

"Not today, sir," I answered.

"Well, what do you want?"

"I have a lead on some early copper and I need your advice."

"Early American copper?"

"American as apple pie," I replied.

In response the black iron gate across the front door clicked slightly and popped open.

Silver greeted me in the same baggy pants and cardigan he had worn the day I had visited him with Unity. But the clothes looked cleanly pressed, and I had a fleeting fantasy of an upstairs closet containing row after row of identical outfits.

"You sure your auntie's not around?" he said, craning his neck past me and glancing up and down the street.

"She was busy." I flashed him a smile.

"Nazi car," he said, nodding at the Mercedes.

I waited for a remark about aboriginal chauffeurs, but none came, and we went into the house.

"I've been looking at draped-bust cents," I began, mentioning the coin I had heard Hamilton request from Pinipaldi. "But I don't feel confident about the coins and the prices. Can you tell me about the market? Maybe give me the name of some reliable dealers?"

"The only reliable dealers are collectors," he said. "If the person you buy from doesn't love coins—doesn't have some of his own put away—find another source. Your man's just in it for a quick buck and probably doesn't know coins. Tomorrow he could be selling soy beans."

"Do large-cent prices go up and down much?"

"I don't pay attention to prices. I don't buy so much now."

"What could make the prices go up sharply?"

"Why are you asking me these questions?"

"I don't want to pay too much."

"Ah shaddap, Mr. Nazi limousine. You got plenty of money."

I didn't know what I was after, exactly. There had to be some reason why Hamilton would have asked Pinipaldi to counterfeit the particular coins he mentioned, but I wasn't getting the information from Silver.

"Is a 1799 cent a good one to have?" I asked.

"You want to make money in coins, do your homework," the old man responded.

He pushed his easy chair back and seemed to focus on a spot on the ceiling. "Now, then, there are three known varieties of the 1799 large cent. Two started out as 1798 cents and were restruck—"

"Restruck?"

He looked annoyed. "The blank, the planchet, in this case purchased from an English company called Boulton and Watt, but later produced domestically, is struck by the die in the mint. That's what makes the imprint. Anyway, they didn't use all the 1798 cents. In 1799 they still had some. So they used the old ones to create the new by stamping a new date over the old one. Too bad they can't do that with old men, no?"

I smiled and he continued.

"Some were also struck on clean planchets. Like I said, three types. None of them are common."

"I heard a handful were coming into the market."

"We're not talking transistor radios here," he snorted. "There's no such thing as a handful. Some copper was hoarded for its metal value, but those hoards have all been unearthed by now. I'd be surprised if there were ten good examples of all three varieties in the world today."

"Ten!"

"That's why we call them rare coins," Silver said with the tiniest hint of a smile. "I happen to have an example of the rarest variety. Would you like to see it?"

Before I could tell him that I was only asking because I was on the track of a murderer, he toddled off into another room, leaving me sitting surrounded by dark wood, Tiffany lamps and the nagging sense that for every step of catch-up I managed, Harry Hamilton jumped ahead by two.

The coin, when it finally arrived, was extraordinary. It was bright and red and essentially unmarked, and Silver assured me that it was as it had been when new. There was a wreath on one side, and a lady in a low-cut blouse with her hair tied back with a ribbon on the other.

"Big tits, eh?" Silver cackled.

He made me handle it wearing white cotton gloves.

It was almost five o'clock when I made it to the Wall Street address on Harry Hamilton's card. Waku pulled up outside and I rang Tibbet from the Benz. He sounded anxious when he heard I was outside, but I went in anyway.

The lobby of the building was of the sort my attorneys had told me should greet visitors to the Dark Foundation. There was a high, domed ceiling decked in tile and awash with yellow light from several crystal chandeliers. The floors were marble and the doormen and elevator men all wore matching brown uniforms with yellow braids. There were two plain-clothes private cops at the magazine stand at the far end of the lobby, trying to look nonchalant but spending too long choosing gum.

From his name and voice, I expected Tibbet to look like a retired British postal clerk. Instead, I was greeted by a fresh-faced man in his middle twenties with a thick shock of brown hair and wingtips to match.

"I'm Timothy Tibbet," he said, shaking my hand. "I'm afraid Harry Hamilton is still out of the office."

"Have you been able to reach him?" I asked.

"I'm sorry, no. But let's get started anyway. Mr. Hamilton can take over when he returns."

I sat down in a leather chair that matched Tibbet's shoes and leaned forward.

"I'll tell you, Tim," I began. "I'm no numismatist. I'm just interested in making money."

"Yes, Mr. Dark. I understand. Making money. That's what we're here to do, sir."

"What makes the market rise and fall?"

"Supply and demand," he replied. "Rare coins are eminently collectible. Have been for thousands of years. The supply of high-quality material is limited, and as more people want the coins, the prices rise. We invest the fund's money in a portfolio of such rare coins. You never actually own a particular coin."

"How are the prices determined?"

"By coin dealers nationwide communicating on a computer network. Bids are posted, as are asking prices of coins for sale."

"Like a gigantic electronic bulletin board? Like commodities?"

"Commodities are more speculative," Tibbet replied. "If you bid electronically, you are bound to buy if someone agrees to your price."

"And prices rise when somebody raises the bid?"

"Of course."

"So if you knew a certain ultra-rare coin wasn't available, you could drive up the price by offering more than you were willing to pay then, right? Then, if you suddenly managed to get hold of the coin in question cheaply, you'd be way ahead. If I remember correctly from economics class, that would be called 'making a market.' Sounds like it's easy to do with coins."

Tibbet seemed a bit rattled, but he gave me his best reassuring-salesman smile.

"Actually, Mr. Dark, sir, we've found this marketplace to be honest and cooperative. Besides, people don't just 'introduce' ultra-rarities into the marketplace. These things weren't made yesterday."

"Hamilton must be a real expert," I said, biting my tongue.

"Actually, sir, Mr. Hamilton specializes in silver United States government issues. I buy most of the gold for the fund."

"You mean Hamilton doesn't know anything that much about gold?"

Tibbet retrenched. "Mr. Hamilton is extremely knowledgeable, sir. It's just that numismatics is a big field. People tend to specialize."

"What about coins from other countries?" I asked, certain I was on to something but not sure what it was.

"The bottom line is the collector base," said

Tibbet. "That's what makes the portfolio rise. There just aren't enough fanciers of foreign coinage to stabilize the market in the United States. At least not yet."

"So you're pretty conservative?"

"With an aggressive edge." Tibbet smiled again, showing sharp white teeth.

Chapter 33

ARNET PICHAUD WORE hand-tailored English suits and silk Italian neckties, and smelled—appropriately enough—like a French whore. He was richer than a mythical king, and unlike me, he looked the part.

Arnet lived mostly in a ground-floor triplex in Manhattan, accessible only from the lobby and appearing to be the door to a fire hose cabinet. Doormen in his building were well-taken care of, ensuring that even occupants of the other twelve floors of the building had no idea that the billionaire financier resided beneath them.

And if they had known, the name would likely have meant nothing to them. Pichaud was the sort of man whose role in world events could only be deduced posthumously, and then only by a truly determined investigative historian, one willing to wade through reams of personal correspondence, private banking records and descriptions of corporate proceedings written purposely in incomprehensible legalese. Although he was a personal advisor to presidents and prime ministers, his name was never in a newspaper, and was rarely mentioned—at least in any geopolitical connection—at even the ritziest of cocktail parties. Pichaud didn't own planes or trains or boats or oil fields or philanthropic foundations. Pichaud made deals. And he had made them for Uncle Andrew.

I hated to ask Arnet a favor, since I was sure to live to regret it, but he was certainly the man to skewer Harry Hamilton's career, and I went to see him at the Yale Club. The place was perfect for Pichaud, a house that worshiped brainpower, and located right behind Grand Central Station.

"I know why you like this place," I said as I approached his shining pate from behind.

"Why?" he asked, not bothering to turn around.

"Because smart people come here and the railroad tracks are so close," I said. "It's like a constant reminder that if you can't outthink 'em, you can always outrun 'em."

"I can always outthink them," he replied, taking a swig of port from a delicate crystal snifter.

"Part of outthinking them is to have an escape hatch."

He smiled. "And Andrew said you didn't have a head for business."

"Little early for booze, no?" I said, sitting down.

"I knew I was meeting you."

"Very funny. Nice suit. Liberty tie?"

"Hermès," he answered. "Now what do you need?"

"I need to hang a guy until the crows pick at his bones."

"You're vulgar," he said, wrinkling his nose in distaste and taking a long cigarette out of a thin gold vest-pocket case.

"So I've been told."

"Wall Street?"

I named the firm.

He cringed.

"I hope you're not doing business with *them*. Their balance sheet's terrible. They're available cheap, but even the British won't touch them. Even the Japanese, and you know how they love a name. How come you like this guy so much?"

"It's personal."

"Ah, it's personal. You going to tell me about it?"

"He's a killer. He's ruthless."

"Why not go to the police?"

"No proof."

"And you want him yourself."

I nodded.

"New money's so dangerous." He shook his head.

I leaned forward so far I could smell his breath. It was smoky and stale. He met my stare unfazed.

"I don't want him to be able to borrow a quarter for a phone call," I said. "I don't want anyone with fifty cents to let him in the door."

"And about the killing?"

"I'll take care of that."

Arnet let his pudgy form sink back into the armchair.

"No way to connect me?"

"Never met you."

"I love to help thugs," he muttered.

"I'm not a thug."

"Why can't you do this yourself? You've got the financial muscle. I hear more and more about you all the time. You even cost me some money lately, that shopping center deal with the Saudis."

"That was *yours*?" I asked incredulously. "I thought some Brazilian banker was putting it together."

"Morera. Works for me. Majority shares in that bank."

"Why didn't you tell me?"

"I was proud of you. You got a deal. Now why don't you just handle this the same way?"

"I need to stay low. Can't let him trace it back to me. He's smart."

"And what's in it for me?"

"Robotics," I said.

"Forget it," he said. "The Japanese control the field."

"That's what they think," I said. "You ever hear of 'smart cars'?"

Pichaud shook his bald head.

"How about NASA?"

He sat forward and rubbed his fat hands together. It amazed me that his palms could get that close with all those rings on his fingers.

Chapter 34

ARNET ASKED ME to lunch, but I declined, hoping it wasn't too late to invite Isabelle for some bread-breaking on neutral ground. I walked back to the office and found Waku lounging in the reception area.

"Don't lounge," I said. "I don't like to see you lounging."

"I can't be working back there right now, Detective." He gestured to the interior with his head. "Isabelle's making war. You have got to tell that lady from California to stop calling here."

Isabelle was wearing a sleeveless chiffon blouse and a purple skirt. She was engrossed in a computer spreadsheet and barely looked up when I walked in.

"Your little bird from California called again," she said. "The number is on your desk."

I grabbed the back of her chair and spun her around.

"She's not my little bird, all right? And she's calling because your friend Harry Hamilton murdered her boss."

"I suppose I should be flattered that jealousy and remorse have driven you to this level of fantasy," she said.

I pursed my lips and blew air.

"I'm not kidding, Isabelle. And I really need to find out where he is."

"Good luck," she replied, swiveling around and putting her fingers back on the computer keys.

Boiling, I went into my office and called Morgan.

"The police have been here," she said.

"Did you mention Hamilton?"

"No. I have no proof he's involved, and I didn't want to admit to eavesdropping and then have to answer all kinds of questions about you and me."

"That's withholding evidence," I said.

"Yeah, well, then why don't you come back out here and tell them yourself?"

"I plan to," I said. "Just not yet."

"I figured that. Look, I need your help. Michael left a mess here, I mean financially, and I have to clean it up. Clients are calling in from all over the place."

"Why don't you just walk away?"

She was silent for a moment.

"I can't do that," she said at last. "I'm a partner."

"You need a lawyer?"

"I don't need a lawyer, Nestor. I want to make this business go, and I can, with a little cash. Do you mind if you don't get your hundred thousand back right away?"

So that was what the call was about. My fingers cooled around the receiver.

"Certainly I mind. It's foundation money."

"What if I send you your coins?"

"I was paying for Michael's expertise, and for his ongoing services."

"Listen," said Morgan, her voice tight with desperation, "I would have been the one to choose the coins anyhow. And I *will* manage them for you. I'm trying to work it out so there's a gallery here to do that six months, a year from now. I'll send you coins worth four times what you've paid if you just float me now."

"Four times?"

"I'll send you good coins, Nestor. Worth four hundred thousand at least."

"You're on," I said.

I hung up and buzzed Isabelle on the intercom.

"Lunch?"

"I beg your pardon?"

"Are you free for lunch?"

"I don't think so," she said.

"You have other plans?"

"I'm on a diet."

"*Samosas?* A little *saag paneer*?" I asked, hoping to entice her with promises of Indian dumplings and spinach.

"I thought you had to find a killer."

"I'm begging," I said.

"Begging happens out here, on your knees, by my desk." She hung up.

While she was waiting, and I knew damn well she *was* waiting, Waku walked into my office.

"I think you should beg her. She's worth it. I won't tell."

I was still giving him the how-the-hell-do-you-know-about-this look when he smiled and tugged on his ear. "Bushman ears," he said.

In response, I took the Charlotte dollar out of my desk drawer and handed it to him.

"Return this to Mr. Tibbet on Wall Street," I said. "Right into his hand. Just tell him that it's from me. Nothing else. Got it?"

Then I got down on my knees and waddled out to Isabelle's office.

From my perspective down by the floor, Isabelle's quarters looked no more modest than my own.

"Nice digs you've got here," I said.

She was busy at her computer, sitting behind her large rosewood desk, and she didn't even look up.

"Rosewood is from the tropical rain forest," I said. "It's an endangered hardwood."

"And I'm ashamed you bought it for me," she replied, her nose still to the computer screen. "But since it's been chopped down and rendered incapable of producing oxygen for people and other living things, I feel okay about putting it to good use. Are you here to beg?"

"I'm a bad beggar," I said, waddling closer to her knees.

"Get better," she said, glancing at me. "It breeds character, something you have in remarkably short supply."

"I don't exactly know what I'm apologizing for," I began. "But I'm sorry."

"That was a terrible beginning," she said, her beautiful green eyes flicking back to the screen.

"I'm sorry for taking another woman out on a date," I said, pressing my torso against her warm knees.

"Getting warmer." She studied the screen ever more intently, then made some rapid taps on the keys. "But still not on the money."

"I'm sorry for being out of touch overnight."

"Getting colder," she said.

I stood up and pulled her roughly from her chair. She resisted, but I cupped her perfect white chin in my palms and turned her face toward me.

"I'm sorry for lying to you. It won't happen again."

"Ever?" She had her hands on my chest, palms to me, pushing me away, but not really. She was looking deep into my eyes.

I shook my head.

"No more Morgan Pajaro?"

"I have to see her again, about the murder, but strictly business. But you've got to promise me to stay away from Hamilton until I can bring him down. He's a killer."

"We'll talk about that at lunch."

The Indian maître d' was completely unimpressed by my name.

"Indians are spiritual people," Isabelle whispered in my ear. "They aren't impressed by money."

While we waited for our food, I cautiously circled the subject of Harry Hamilton.

"How do you know he killed Pinipaldi?" Isabelle asked after I had related what I could of the story without confessing to the tryst with Morgan. "You didn't see it, did you?"

"He assaulted the guy and threatened to kill him. A couple of days later he's dead. Hell of a coincidence, wouldn't you say?"

"That's exactly what it sounds like, Mr. Policeman, and of all people, you should know."

"Did you sleep with him?"

"I can't imagine that's any of your business."

The waiter showed up with the *samosas*, dark brown sweet-and-sour tamarind chutney, a red pepper mash and a spicy mint sauce.

I took a teaspoon of the spicy mint sauce, dribbled it over a *samosa* and took a bite.

"How long are you going to punish me?" I said.

"You've got a lot to learn about women, buddy boy," she answered.

Chapter 35

I WENT TO Amos Larsen's dojo after lunch.

"You look soft," Amos remarked as I walked in the door.

"Just relaxing before battle," I told him, heading for the changing room.

He came in and watched me get dressed, standing in the doorway with his massive arms crossed over his chest.

"Who are you fighting?"

I shrugged, pulled my workout clothes on and headed for the heavy bag. He followed me quietly and watched me move. I started slow, tapping the canvas with straight, darting Wing Chung punches until he moved in to where the bag was and traded blows with me in rhythmic fashion, blocking and parrying as I drove for his face and midsection, returning the favor with hands the size of wine barrels.

"You here because you need me?" he asked.

"I'm here because I need this," I grunted, dodging

a particularly vicious rising kick from one of his size-thirteen feet.

"Want to tell me about it?"

Suddenly I realized that I did, so slowly, gaspingly, while we continued to trade blows, I related Hamilton's deception.

It took time, and when I was finished, Amos withdrew from fighting range, bowed and shook his thick blond ponytail.

"So what do you want to do?" he asked.

"Hurt him bad."

"You could go to Rignola now, with what you know."

"I have nothing that would stand up in court. I heard the guy confess to a felony. I heard him assault and threaten a man who wound up dead. Compelling, but not convincing. I lost too many busts that way when I was on the street. It's my word against his. I want him in a leakproof bag."

"Why?"

"I led him right to the guy he killed. He duped me."

"And?"

"And he fucked Isabelle."

He nodded slowly.

We practiced until my heart was in my ears and my limbs felt like lead and I knew what I had to do.

Chapter 36

THE NEXT MORNING Isabelle came into my office carrying a Federal Express package the size of a shoebox.

"It's from your little bird at Tangible Scarcities," she said. "I had to sign for it."

Instead of rising to the bait, I took the package and slit open the tape with a custom-made, Damascus-steel fighting knife I kept in the desk.

There were coins inside, and a note.

"May I read that aloud to you?" Isabelle asked, reaching for the scented blue parchment weave.

I let her take it.

" 'Dear Mr. Dark,' " she began. "I like that. Very professional. No first names. She's discreet, I'll give you that."

"Just read."

" 'Enclosed please find the investment portfolio selection the gallery has made for you,' " Isabelle continued. " 'We recommend a minimum investment period of eighteen months, but should you wish to liquidate your holdings prior to that time, we will be happy to assist you. Like all our clients, you can expect to hear from us should any unexpected developments occur in the rate-coin marketplace. Sincerely, Morgan Pajaro, Director.' Director. Wow. She sure doesn't waste any time."

"You can say that again," I muttered.

"Screw you."

There were five gold pieces in the box, and I recognized them to be fine representatives of the major United States series.

"This is the 1848 California gold quarter eagle," I told Isabelle, holding up one of the coins and hoping to impress her with my book learning. "Fewer than fourteen hundred were minted."

Isabelle looked like she couldn't care less.

"And this," I continued, holding another of the coins aloft, "is an 1899 proof gold eagle. Only eighty-six made."

The telephone interrupted me. It was Unity.

"Ron Silver asked me over," she said. I could see her blush through the wire. "I wondered if you'd go along."

"You want me to chaperone you? Shall I bring a gun?"

"Just stop it," she said. "Why can't you be a gentleman about this?"

"Seriously, Unity, I think it's safe to have a date with the old man."

"He's not that old, and it's not a date. Now, will you go with me or not?"

I was on the way to pick up Unity when Isabelle reached me on the cellular phone in the Benz and patched through a call from Timothy Tibbet.

"I received the gold piece you sent over with your chauffeur," he said.

"Yes?"

"May I ask where you got it?"

"You should recognize it," I said. "It's from your portfolio. Harry Hamilton sent it to me as a sample," I lied.

"When was this?"

"Yesterday. We talked on the phone."

"Did he say where he was?"

"No. I just told him I was interested in the fund and he sent that along. He said it was very rare."

"It certainly is."

"Will it make me money?"

"Of course."

"I'd like to talk to Mr. Hamilton about it when he returns to the office."

"So would I," Tibbet muttered. "I'll have him call you."

Unity's living room smelled of dried-flower pot-pourri and unfamiliar herbs. There were crumpets on fine china dishes on doilies on the coffee table in front of her, and she held her rose quartz orb in her lap, massaging it unconsciously with hands too smooth for her age.

"Honestly, you're just like a little girl," I told her. "You can speak to Mr. Silver yourself."

"You don't realize the effect I have on men," she replied, twinkling.

"You're so wrong," I moaned. "Besides, I've been back to see him once already and he doesn't like my Nazi car."

"Did you do something to antagonize him?"

"He doesn't like my coin questions. I think they're

intellectually disappointing to him. Anyway, I've brought along some gold pieces to show him. I got them from a dealer in California."

"You're making me go out too much lately, Nestor, you know that? I don't like to go out."

Pynchon held Unity's mink for her when we got to the foyer. I couldn't bring myself to remind her that *she* had summoned *me* because *she* wanted to go out.

"You don't need the coat, Unity. It's summer outside."

"You'll use the air conditioner in the Nazi car?" she asked.

"Not if you don't want me to."

"I do want you to. That's why I'm wearing my fur."

I looked at Pynchon, hoping for a small smile, some eye contact, anything that would ally us in the face of such complete female illogic. I got nothing but an impassive stare.

Waku drove us to Silver's house with the air-conditioning set to "Arctic." Unity seemed happy in her fur. I sat with my teeth clenched to keep from shivering.

I got out of the car first, leaving Unity in midwinter while I rang Silver's bell.

"It's Nestor Dark again, sir," I said.

"You? You talk too much. I'm busy. Go away. Take your Nazi car and drive."

"My aunt Unity is with me," I said. "She's waiting in the car."

"Come on up," said Silver.

Unity and I climbed the stairs to the brownstone arm in arm. The sixth sense which abounds in every successful policeman made me glance upward, and when I did I caught a glimpse of movement in the window.

"It's working," I told Unity. "He's watching us."

The visit went far more smoothly than the previous one. Silver led us into his living room without a word and settled comfortably on the couch, patting it in anticipation of feeling Unity next to him. She looked inquiringly at me and I gave her an encouraging nod. She sat down beside Silver. We all stared at each other. I took out the box of coins that Morgan had sent me in hopes of breaking the ice.

"I bought these coins to start my collection," I said.

Silver was smiling at Unity. He took her hand.

I cleared my throat. "There are some real rarities here."

For a guy obsessed with coins, Silver showed remarkably little interest.

"There's an 1848 quarter eagle and an 1899 eagle in proof," I ventured.

He looked up.

"There were only eighty-six of those eagles minted," I continued, gaining confidence.

"Don't tell me about minted. I know all about minted. I have one of those coins. Now let me see that."

He rose from his seat on the couch and snagged the coin from my hand.

"Very pretty," he murmured, rapidly turning the plastic slab over and over in the room's dim light. I don't know how he could see a thing.

"What else you got?" he asked, apparently having lost all interest in Unity.

I gave him the rest of Morgan's coins and he took

the box to his desk, where he turned on a highly concentrated white light attached to a magnifying viewer.

At first he stood bent over them, grunting and groaning and turning one coin after another over in his hairy hands. After a time, seeming to have forgotten that we were there at all, he sat down and started mumbling to himself. He opened a drawer and withdrew a jeweler's loupe.

Unity motioned me over to the couch, and I sat down beside her.

"Why'd you have to bring those coins?" she asked in a quiet, angry voice.

Before I had a chance to apologize, Silver stood up. He wore a broad smile.

"I pass your test, Mr. Dark, ha ha!"

"What are you talking about?"

"Every one of them is a fake!"

Chapter 37

I WAS TOO stunned to speak. Silver approached me, his hands outstretched and full of the slabbed coins, all in a jumble, like an offering of rice.

"This is why you asked me about the Turk, right? To test me?"

I stood frozen as he dumped the coins into my hands.

"You want I should tell you the whole story?" He grinned at me. His teeth looked like gray marbles.

I nodded dumbly.

"First I looked at them and I thought to myself that the strikes are a bit too clean, you know, the edges and the definition and everything. Then I noticed some other little things, like on this one . . ."

He pointed to a coin, but I couldn't take my eyes off his face.

". . . there's a little bit of metal, like a burr, along the Indian's neck. That shouldn't be there when you have a well-worn die."

I held up my hand to interrupt him.

"When was this counterfeiting done?"

"I can only say for sure that they are not original. Probably somebody made them not too long ago. Maybe last year, two, three years ago, but I'm just guessing. Somebody made them for investors, thinking maybe the people who put them in plastic don't know so much and maybe they wouldn't see the little bird."

"The little bird?" I whispered, my throat suddenly dry as the air at 30,000 feet.

"I told you already, every counterfeiter likes to sign his work. Look here." He took me over to his desk and held one of the coins beneath his magnifying light. "Take a close look."

I looked but I really couldn't see anything.

"Closer," he insisted, pressing me down. He pushed the magnifying lamp aside and thrust his pocket magnifier between my eye and the coin. The seemingly smooth surface of the gold piece jumped into radical relief.

"There," he said, pointing to what appeared to be no more than a tiny dot on the left side of the coin.

"I don't see . . ." I began.

Exasperated, he pulled another loupe from the drawer.

"Twenty power," he said. "Now look."

I looked again under the higher magnification, and there, revealed in all its infinitesimal glory, was a tiny bird with outstretched wings.

"It's flying," I murmured.

And my stomach churned as I suddenly understood what a complete fool I'd been.

Charlie Bender asked me up for cocktails that night in honor of Kevin Dilley. He wouldn't give me the details, but I smelled the perfumed hand of Arnet Pichaud at work. Bender lived in an old apartment building on Riverside Drive in the high nineties. The neighborhood wasn't the best, but it wasn't the worst either. Even college professors as smart as Bender don't make enough money to live hog-high in New York.

But there was a doorman, and the ceilings were as high as a cathedral's, and with a little imagination one could envision upper-class ladies of the 1850's strolling with parasols in hand perhaps looking down off the high banks of the Hudson River across to the New Jersey Palisades as horses and buggies clopped by. Early in my career with the NYPD, I had been a beat cop in the Heights. I had been flushed with excitement at the romance of it all until one day I had to shoot a drug-wild pusher in the park. He had fallen over the stone retaining wall and ended up a floater in the Hudson, taking with him the bullet from my .38 service revolver and all my dreams of days golden and long past.

Bender's quarters were as cluttered as those of the mad scientist in any B movie, but that night they seemed even closer because at least thirty people were milling about. The long benches in the living room, which normally bore inventions in various states of completion, were covered with catered goodies lit by halogen lamps.

"You shouldn't put halogen lights on onion dip," I bent and whispered in Charlie's ear. "The heat makes the edges go brown."

"It doesn't do wonders for smoked salmon either," he retorted, "but it sure makes that oily skin glow!"

I rolled my eyes.

"You gonna tell me why I'm here?" I asked.

"Kevin's had an offer. A Brazilian bank has stepped in and offered to bankroll him for the NASA project and also for the auto guidance system."

"A Brazilian bank?"

"Just due diligence ahead," said Dilley, appearing magically next to Bender's elbow.

The three of us retired into Bender's study to talk. The room was so crammed with computer equipment and books that I was forever amazed the old floor didn't simply collapse.

"Beams," said Bender. "This building was constructed in the days of solid hardwood beams."

Dilley smiled. "I guess I won't be needing to talk to your lawyers," he said.

"My loss. Congratulations."

Dilley beamed.

"Let's introduce Nestor to Twiggy," said Bender, pushing a button on the side of his wheelchair. A moment later a device resembling a stock pot with the high hips and long legs of an ostrich ambled out from between two bookcases. I didn't like the way it was closing in on me.

"What is it?" I asked, stepping back as it drew nearer.

"She's a prototype for one of my security robots," Dilley explained. "Charlie did the A.I. We call her Twiggy for her wonderful wasp waist."

"She looks like a pig on stilts to me."

"Thanks a lot," said Twiggy, the sound issuing forth from somewhere deep in her cauldron-shaped "torso," but sounding surprisingly human.

"What's she doing now?"

"She's coming to shake hands," Bender informed me pleasantly as the robot reached a spot in front of my feet and extended its claw.

We shook hands timorously. She responded with light and gentle pressure.

"Twiggy, there's an intruder at the door!" Bender said suddenly and with great urgency.

The robot swiveled around slightly until two V-shaped slots on her "chest" were aimed at the door.

"I don't think so, Dr. Bender," she intoned. "I detect neither infrared radiation, movement nor a change in the material density of the door that would suggest that a human being is standing on the other side of it."

"Can't fool *her*," Bender said with paternal satisfaction.

"Why would you want to?" Twiggy asked.

"To demonstrate the sophistication of your logic circuits and engrams," Charlie replied.

I needed to tell Bender about Morgan and Pinipaldi and Hamilton, but this was clearly not the time. The smell of pâté and smoked salmon was seeping under the door, and the babble of voices outside was growing louder by the minute. Someone slammed a hand on the door.

"Come on, Kev," came a half-drunken voice. "Forget business for an hour! Let's party!"

"My public," Dilley said sheepishly.

A moment later the door burst open and a burly man wearing a leather vest peeked in.

"Can't have this," he rumbled, stepping inside and making for Dilley. "Just can't have it. Sorry, gentlemen, but the man of the hour is going with me."

He reached up and grabbed the new millionaire playfully by the neck, steering him toward the door.

"Careful!" Bender warned.

But the man was awash with enthusiasm and bourbon, and he continued to propel Dilley toward the party.

"Nestor," Bender began.

Before I could do anything, Twiggy was racing for what she imagined to be Dilley's assailant. At first Dilley was amused.

"It's all right, Twiggy," he said.

But Bender wasn't smiling, and when Dilley saw that, he sobered up and tried to wrest his friend's hand from his neck.

"You gotta let go, Ralph," he said. "The robot . . ."

I could see what was coming next. That claw had extended toward Ralph's patella, and Twiggy was moving faster than anything that looked like a stock pot had a right to. I glanced at Bender and saw him frantically pushing buttons on the side of his wheelchair. An innocent man was about to be crippled.

I dived for her hip joint with my ballpoint.

"Don't!" Bender screamed. "She's charged!"

But I was committed. Ralph laughed as Dilley tried to twist free.

My slide got me within range, and I thrust my pen hard into the exposed joint. There was a shower of sparks at the tip, but the pen held, freezing the joint and unbalancing the robot. She toppled, her claw opening and closing desperately, just inches short of Ralph's knee.

"Jesus," said Dilley. "What happened?"

"Time for a drink, Kevin boy," said Ralph from the doorway.

Bender stared at the upended robot unhappily.

"How much current in her shock?" I asked, standing and dusting off my trousers.

"You don't want to know," said Bender in a quavering voice.

"How 'bout a Carlsberg?" Dilley proposed, trying hard to lighten things up. "We got some especially for you."

I declined.

I need to keep my senses sharp.

Chapter 38

ALTHOUGH HE WAS always more than kind and even-handed with me, in business Andrew Dark's relaxed persona was replaced with a rapacious appetite for money, success and the utter annihilation of the competition.

One evening, some two years before he died, I arrived at the Redding house to find the furniture pushed up against the wall to make room for a scale model of a real estate development. Uncle Andrew was pacing back and forth before it, running his hands through his thinning hair and muttering. He didn't notice me until I was on the other side of the expanse of white cardboard.

"Ah. Hello, Nestor," he said.

"What is this?" I gestured at the model.

"It was to be a new resort in the South Pacific. It's about to become the ruin of a man's life."

"Want to tell me about it?"

"The island is overrun by sea birds." He sighed heavily. "Of course, we didn't know that when the proposal came in for the development money. I was behind the consortium that went for it. Plans looked good, air routes wére there, land was dirt-cheap, beautiful water, beautiful beaches, available work force, raw materials, everything. We anted up ten percent of the projected fifty million . . ."

I blanched.

"Earnest money, that's all. To let him know we were serious."

"Five million dollars just to let him know you're serious?"

"Most of that's gone," Uncle Andrew replied. "Along with the developer. My people tell me he's in Macao now."

"Macao!"

"The birds fly to one side of the island and they shit there. They leave the other side alone. Nobody knew that the development site was covered in three inches of guano."

"What are you going to do?"

"He's using a Macao bank." Uncle Andrew winked. "A Portuguese bank, naturally. The Portuguese still control Macao."

"So?"

"I'm a shareholder."

"In the bank?"

My uncle nodded with a smile. "I've arranged for the transfer of some funds."

"His funds?"

"Not for long." Uncle Andrew's eyes twinkled.

I was shocked. This was a new side to Andrew Dark.

"You shouldn't be telling me this."

Uncle Andrew looked suddenly annoyed. "Because you're a cop? I should think a cop would understand payback. He's got money beyond the five million in that bank, and I'm wiring all of it out."

He glanced at his watch.

"In an hour, bird shit is all he'll have left."

"But by doing this you're no better than he is!"

"The hell I'm not! I didn't intentionally defraud a group of investors, I simply recovered my assets and punished him for trifling with me. What I've done here is to pay a man back *in kind*. That's the best sort of revenge."

The morning after the party for Dilley, I took Tolstoy for a walk in the woods to think about revenge. The sun was just up, and the dew was still dripping from the trees and clinging to the grass underfoot. My shoes got wet, and bits of cut grass clung to Tolstoy's nose. I inhaled the summer smells deeply, and walked through the forest with my eyes closed, trying to extend my chi and use it as a blind man might use a swaying cane. I succeeded for a time, the sound of Tolstoy's breathing telling me he was still trotting happily alongside, until I became conscious of my success, and with that awareness the trance was gone, the tool was lost and I walked straight into the peeling bark of a birch tree.

Suddenly it was all so simple.

"Time to go home," I told Tolstoy, bending down to pat his thick head at his disappointed expression. He looked like he needed a talking-to, so I gave him one.

"There's nothing I can do to bring Michael Pinipaldi back," I continued, Tolstoy's eyes watching my face. "And I'm not a killer, so I can't pay Harry Hamilton back in kind. Still, I think I know a way to recover my assets and dish out a little punishment on the side."

He smiled and wagged his tail happily, as if he understood, and then ducked down and came up with a mouthful of something that once was a rabbit.

I got to the office by eight, and the first thing I did was phone Sam Houser at the *Wall Street Journal*. Houser and I had known each other since the day Uncle Andrew died. He had disturbed me in my grief, and I had told him so, but he had been eager to portray my uncle in a positive light, and unlike so many reporters—who will promise anything for a fact they can twist—he had done so. Houser had done much for my image over the years, was an honest writer and deserved a hot story.

"The august Mr. Dark," he said when he picked up the phone.

"It's just July," I said. "And what are you doing at work so early?"

"And so clever! What can I do for you?"

"Ask not what you can do for the Dark," I intoned. "But what the Dark can do for you."

"You got a story for me?" he asked, trying to conceal his excitement.

"What do you know about rare-coin mutual funds?"

He immediately named a couple of firms, Harry Hamilton's among them.

"Hamilton's selling counterfeit coins," I said.

"What!! I don't believe it."

"Believe it. They're encased in plastic, but they're fakes."

"You can prove this?"

"No, *you* can prove it. You're the reporter. And you've already forgotten where you heard this."

"All right, all right. Give me something to go on."

"Arrange for a look at his inventory. Get a real expert, like someone from the museum, to go along, because these are brilliant fakes. You got a pencil?"

"Go," said Houser.

"Check out an 1849 Charlotte gold dollar, and I believe he will shortly have a proof 1899 gold eagle and an 1848 quarter eagle, too. Some other early gold as well. All counterfeit."

"How'd you find out about all this, Nestor?"

"Just dumb luck," I said. I hung up and went into the toy room for a few blissful hours with my Feinwerkbau air rifle and the tiny black dot at the end of the room.

Arnet Pichaud called just after two P.M.

"That Dilley deal is a sweetheart, Nestor. The man is a genius."

"I know," I said. "I met some of his work last night."

"The word is out on your friend Hamilton," he said. "He's finished."

"Thank you kindly. And, Arnet? The Dilley thing? Will you consider us square on the Saudi shopping-center deal, too? Honestly, I didn't know they were your Brazilian bankers."

Laughing, he agreed and hung up.

"Arnet was calling about Harry, wasn't he?" Isabelle asked, walking into the room.

"Harry?"

"Look, Nestor, I'm not feeling like I trust you that much right now. You better stop playing games and tell me what's going on."

"I tried to tell you about Hamilton," I countered, motioning for her to sit down. "You didn't listen."

She remained standing and looked me squarely in the eye. "I listened. You just didn't convince me. Now, why don't you tell me everything, from beginning to end. And while you're at it, why don't you tell me the truth about Morgan Pajaro?"

So I told her. I started slowly, pacing back and forth in front of the window that looked out on the summer crowds walking down Fifth Avenue. I related how Hamilton had approached me, how he had duped me, about the trail to Santa Barbara. I told her about Morgan's coins, about Silver. I told her what I had in mind.

"You're going to sell him the fakes?" she said slowly.

I nodded. "I'm going to try to trap him with the counterfeits."

"But you still don't *know* he killed Pinipaldi!"

"I know he's a crook. I heard him try to buy counterfeit coins."

"From a man you told him was a counterfeiter."

"I didn't tell him so! I told him I was suspicious. I told him I needed more time to investigate."

"Very enjoyable investigations, from what I can gather," Isabelle said, smoothing her skirt and fiddling with the buttons on her blouse. "And now you find that your lover was the counterfeiter all along."

"Isabelle, please. I'm so sorry. I was duped."

"Duped into the sack, were you?"

"Just like you!" I roared.

"Never."

"What?"

"I was never duped into the sack. I knew exactly what I was doing."

I slumped into my desk chair and looked at her thighs pressed tight against the wood of my desk.

"That was nice, thanks very much."

"Just payback. You started it."

"Well, we'll have to fix it, then, won't we?" I said. "Now will you help me?"

"I will help you," Isabelle said, standing slowly. "But I'm not sure that means things are fixed."

"It's a start."

"Harry Hamilton's got bad skin, Nestor. I wouldn't want to cross him."

At first I thought she was mocking me, repeating something I'd said to her once and forgotten, but the look in her eyes told me she was completely serious.

"What?"

"I figure guys with bad skin have terrible tempers, maybe just because they're angry at the world because they look the way they do."

"Don't worry about his temper. I'll take care of that. I'm going to dial his office now. Are you ready to speak to him?"

She nodded and I turned on the speaker phone and dialed Hamilton's office.

He was in.

"Nestor asked me to get you on the phone," she began. "Why haven't I heard from you?"

"I've been out of town, doll." Hamilton's voice boomed over the box. "I just got back."

Only a guy like Hamilton could get away with calling Isabelle Redfield "doll."

"Where were you?"

"I had to go to the Bahamas, retrieve some money from an offshore fund. Am I on a speaker phone?"

"Yes, my hands are busy at the computer. Have you been in the Bahamas the whole time?"

"It's not the easiest thing, doll. There's paperwork. Sometimes things don't go that smoothly, and it meant a lot of money for my firm."

Isabelle didn't say anything, but she didn't have to. Her face was as tight as undersized shoes. Hamilton was the second guy who had lied to her in less than ten days.

"I see," she said. "Anyway, Nestor's been working on your case night and day, traveling around and all. He's giving up."

"Giving up?" He sounded shocked.

"He's a busy man, Harry." She looked at me significantly. "Let me get him for you."

"Hey, wait a minute, doll," Hamilton protested. "When am I going to see you again?"

"I don't know," she answered, and then pushed the hold button.

I reached out for her hand and she let me take it, but it was limp and lifeless.

Chapter 39

"My ASSISTANT TOLD me you called," Hamilton said brightly.

"Where the hell were you? I've been trying to reach you for days."

The front doorbell rang and Isabelle left to answer it.

"Bahamas," said Hamilton. "Business with an offshore account. Took time."

He was a liar, but at least he was a consistent liar.

"Look, I've been calling you to tell you that I can't put any more time into this."

"I understand," said Hamilton.

"I'm sure that Pinipaldi was our man. Too bad we can't arrest him now and get him famous."

"Why not?"

"I thought you'd have heard. He's dead."

"Dead!"

"Shot in the head. They say it was a burglar, maybe trying to rip off some coins."

"My God, that's terrible."

"It ruins all your plans, I know. Listen, I need a small favor in return for the work I did."

"This isn't about your assistant, is it?" Hamilton said cautiously. "I mean, I hope you don't mind. We just got to talking on the phone, you know how it is, and one thing led to another. She's a very beautiful woman."

"Isabelle's personal life is her affair," I said, biting the back of my hand. "The fact is that during the height of poking around for you, I bought some coins at a show in Westchester. They cost me a lot, and because of the way things have turned out, I'd like to get out of them. Would you be interested?"

"Depends on the coins."

I described them.

"Good coins. How much did you pay?"

"I'm into them for three hundred thousand," I said.

Hamilton was silent for a moment.

"Would you be able to send them down?" he asked.

"Right away," I said, and hung up.

At that moment Isabelle stepped in and announced that the elephant delegation had arrived.

"What? I can't see them now!"

"They've brought their new plan," she said.

"A few minutes is all I have," I said. "I'm on my way to take the coins to Hamilton."

Seven feet of intense black man suddenly appeared in the doorway.

"We have worked very hard on a proposal we believe will satisfy your conditions, Mr. Dark."

I gave Isabelle a helpless look and waved him into the office. He was followed by four more tall black men. They made a semicircle behind their leader's chair.

"The idea is incredibly simple," the giant man began in his Oxford accent, "but, I hope you will agree, elegant."

"Go ahead."

"It came to us as a result of the distillation of our socioeconomic situation, which you so readily grasped and communicated," he continued. "You were quite correct when you said that guns and patrols would not solve the problem."

"The gist," I said desperately. "Just give me the gist."

"We're going to hire the poachers to guard the elephants," he said triumphantly.

Even Isabelle was stunned.

The elephant man read our expressions.

"Oh, I know what you're thinking." He smiled. "That this is a poacher's dream come true, to be able to get to the elephants without worry. But remember, they are not poaching because they hate elephants. They are poaching because their families are starving. And poaching is a dangerous and chancy game. They may get shot. They may not find the elephants. The people who buy from them may cheat them. We can put all those variables to rest. We can monitor them as you suggested. They will work for the rangers, under reasonable supervision, and they will work for high wages, thanks to the generous support of the Dark Foundation. And while they are working for a better and steadier wage than they have ever earned before, they will be required to take our ecological and herd education programs. We think this can make a difference."

Isabelle clapped with pleasure.

"You're on for two hundred and fifty thousand," I said, grabbing the man's hand and shaking it. "If it works, there's more. Now please forgive me, but I have an appointment."

I dashed out of the office, stopping only long enough to grab the box of coins and my motorcycle helmet.

"Your jacket!" Isabelle called after me.

I took my private elevator down to where the Paris-Dakar stood waiting, and pressed the starter while I stowed the coins. The big BMW ignited without complaint, but bucked and billowed blue smoke when I guided it up the ramp and out of the garage into the summer midtown heat. The huge front forks compressed and sprang back over the notorious chuckholes of Manhattan as I weaved down Fifth Avenue like a giant kamikaze bumblebee, the bike's black-and-yellow paintwork serving notice to anyone who cared to look in his mirror that if he swerved, he'd be stung.

Parking on Hamilton's section of Wall Street was a challenge, making me wish that I'd had Waku drive me. After circling the block twice and being refused access by three parking lot attendants, I stopped the bike in front of Hamilton's building and put it up on its centerstand. Then I withdrew both the coins and a blue-and-white police placard from the saddlebag and positioned the sign between the controls on the handlebars. Rignola wouldn't be pleased if he knew I was still using the card, stolen from a patrol car on the day I quit the force, but I figured the worst he could do was bust me for impersonating and make Isabelle bail me out.

Helmet tucked under my arm, I walked into Hamilton's plush office suite wearing chinos and carrying coins. The receptionist was an effeminate man in gray pinstripes.

"I'm here to see Mr. Hamilton," I said.

He extended his arms for the coin box.

"I can take that," he said.

"No, you can't."

"We don't allow messengers into the office," he sniffed. "I'm authorized to receive packages."

"Ring Hamilton. Tell him Nestor Dark is waiting," I said calmly.

Lucky for me, Tim Tibbet walked by before I had a replay of Las Vegas.

"Mr. Dark! What a nice surprise!" He shook my hand warmly.

The receptionist stared in astonishment as Tibbet took me by the elbow and escorted me into the bowels of the office.

Hamilton's office looked just like Tibbet's: replete with heavy leather and wood furniture to lend solemnity to the proceedings. Of course, only people of true substance ever got this far into the inner sanctum. The casual investor simply did his paperwork by fax or mail with his broker.

"What a pleasant surprise!" Hamilton said, coming around to shake my hand. "The famous Nestor Dark hawking coins to humble Harry Hamilton."

His desk bore one photo of Hamilton dressed in a blue windbreaker with white trim, standing behind the wheel of a sailboat, his pockmarked face squinting against the spray; and another of him smiling at the camera and holding a golden golf club aloft in his hand. The background was out of focus, but I could just make out palm trees.

"I was going to messenger them down," I said, handing him the box of coins, "but then I decided I'd come and watch while you looked at them, maybe learn something."

He took the box from my hand and sat down at the table. Tibbet stayed by the door until Hamilton dismissed him with a glance.

"It's a shame things didn't work out better," I said. "Your career might have had a real leg up if that guy Pinipaldi hadn't died."

Hamilton shrugged. "Maybe it's better this way. I probably don't have to worry about buying any more fakes."

"And I have to thank you for introducing me to numismatics," I replied.

"If you like coins, maybe you should keep these," said Hamilton, his fingers hovering over the lid of the box. I tried to stay relaxed in my chair and not focus on his hands.

"Ancient coins have really caught my eye. These were an impulse purchase."

"The book before the coin, as they say." Hamilton smiled. "Anyway, I'm pleased you were bitten by the bug. Ancient coins are not my field, but I'm sure Tim Tibbet would be willing to dispense some free advice if you ever need it. He's a real expert."

He opened the box.

"If you don't want those, I'll sell them through a dealer," I said, trying to sound as casual as possible.

Hamilton adjusted the desk lamp so that it shone obliquely on the coins. He turned them rapidly in his hands much the way Silver had. I slipped my palms under my thighs so the sweat wouldn't show.

"I read a little about them," I said, clearing my throat. "They're rare issues. There were only eighty-six of the proof eagles minted."

Hamilton smiled again. "You sure you don't want to start a portfolio? I'd still be happy to help."

"Not right now, thanks."

He lay the coins carefully down in a row on his desk.

"Well?"

"They're very fine coins, Mr. Dark, and I'd very much like to buy them from you for the fund. But . . ." He hesitated. I held my breath.

"Is there a problem?"

"I'm getting a very good deal at three hundred thousand," he said. "You might get more money elsewhere. Stack's Coin Company here in New York could auction them for you. . . ."

"Frankly, I don't have the time for that," I said, standing. "Do you want them or not?"

"I'll have my assistant issue you a check on your way out," he said.

Chapter 40

"HAVE WAKU DEPOSIT this right away," I said, stripping off my helmet and thrusting Hamilton's check into Isabelle's hands. "Call the bank and tell them I have reason to suspect the funds; tell them to put it through immediately."

Isabelle looked at me searchingly.

"He bought them?"

"He bought them."

She nodded slowly. "The Beechcraft Company called about your airplane," she said. "They've delivered it to the Marine Air Terminal at LaGuardia for you. Tamarkin Aviation in Denver will send you the bill."

"It's here? My plane is here?"

Isabelle allowed herself the barest hint of a smile at my excitement.

"And the Nature Conservancy called," she said. "They said a deed and a new survey are on the way, but to tell you that they gratefully accept your offer of land adjacent to the Dark Ranch in Utah."

She followed me into my office.

"Does that mean you're keeping the ranch house?"

"Yes."

"I'm glad. I've always liked it there."

"Would you sit down for a moment?" I asked. "There's something I'd like you to hear."

She sat, and I flicked on the speaker phone and dialed.

"The number for the Federal Trade Commission in Los Angeles, please," I said. "Complaints."

Isabelle watched me closely as I hung up and redialed.

"Federal Trade Commission." A woman's voice came over the speaker. She sounded young and eager. "This is Sheila Gray."

"Do you have a pencil ready, Sheila?" I asked. "I'm about to make your day."

"May I ask who's calling, please?"

"You may ask," I replied, speaking slowly and clearly. "Now write this down. There is a rare-coin gallery up in Santa Barbara. It's called Tangible Scarcities. The director is a woman named Morgan Pajaro. She is also a counterfeiter, and she is selling high-priced counterfeit gold pieces to her clients. Did you get all that?"

"Yes, I did," she answered. "Now may I have your name and address, sir?"

I hung up.

"Is she very beautiful?" Isabelle asked.

I stared at her. "Not like you," I answered finally.

"But there was something hot about her, wasn't there, Nestor? Something you couldn't resist?"

I closed my eyes and thought of Morgan bucking above me, her wild dark hair thrown back, her mouth open, hungry for it all.

"There are things in life I have trouble resisting," I answered after a time. "I'm not sure that all of them are bad for me, but Morgan certainly was. Anyway, it's you I really want, and I am so terribly sorry."

Isabelle got up and left the room.

Two days later Harry Hamilton's name was on the front page of the *Wall Street Journal,* the *New York Times* and a number of smaller papers of specific interest to investors. The police were quoted as saying that they were investigating allegations of fraud, but that no charges had yet been filed. The brokerage house for which he worked had relieved him of all duties. Tim Tibbet was named his successor. It was clear that Harry Hamilton's career was over.

"Does this please you?" Isabelle asked, studying me as I scanned the articles.

"Absolutely," I answered. "He's a crook. I'm surprised they haven't arrested him yet."

"That's the only reason?"

"I thought I'd better keep the rest to myself."

Isabelle started to say something, but the doorbell interrupted her.

"I'll be in the toy room," I said.

I barely had time to load my RWS air rifle with a .177-caliber pellet and take aim at the paper before Isabelle burst into the room. Her hair was mussed and her eyes were wilder than I had ever seen them.

"I'm sorry," she began. "He—"

And Harry Hamilton appeared behind her, a .45 in his hand.

He looked around.

"Quite a little place you have here, Nestor," he said. "Small, cozy. A nest. Nestor's nest." He laughed hysterically. "Fitting that your fantasy life should end here, surrounded by toys."

"What the hell are you doing here?" I demanded, keeping my hand on the rifle and pivoting it almost imperceptibly to bring the muzzle to bear on Hamilton.

"I did a little homework, Nestor boy." He cackled again. "Found out about you and Sam Houser."

"I don't know what you're talking about," I said.

"Bosom buddies, go back five years, you gave him a call about me."

"Sam Houser?" I moved my foot slowly over to the switch that controlled the Z-gauge train transformer.

"Surely a man like you must know the power of the *Wall Street Journal*," he said. "I'll admit that at first I thought it was that bitch Pajaro. Hell of a lay, don't you think? What muscle control! Oh, yes, I fucked her. Just like I fucked your East Coast lady"—he nodded at Isabelle—"but I did it years before you ever met her. So at first I thought she was behind it, knowing what a lowlife she really is, but then I realized this was too subtle, too indirect. Only you would think of it. And over what? A couple of fakes that don't mean anything to you? A sum that you piss out after a night of heavy drinking? Only you had the arrogance, Dark."

"You killed Michael Pinipaldi," Isabelle said, her hand to her mouth, staring at the gun.

"I didn't kill anyone," he said softly. "At least until now."

"I overheard your conversation with Pinipaldi," I said, continuing to pivot the air rifle and moving my foot ever nearer the transformer. "I heard you ask him to make you coins."

"I guess you always believe everything you hear, huh, Nestor? Like you believed me?"

"Nestor's not really much of a detective," Isabelle interjected. "If he ever had the touch, he's lost it now."

Hamilton looked at her in surprise.

The moment his gaze was off me, I touched the transformer switch with my toe, setting my tiny train in motion on the perimeter rail. The movement caught Hamilton's eye and he whirled and fired reflexively.

The slug vaporized the tiny train and sent what had once been precision parts hurtling through the air to penetrate the canvas-and-balsa wings of a beautiful model of a WWI Fokker triplane. The sound of the .45 was deafening, totally masking the report of my air rifle's tiny pellet as it flew across the room at five hundred feet per second, through the light gabardine of Hamilton's trousers and into his left testicle.

Both of Hamilton's arms fell to his groin, and I was on him in an instant. He was big, and strong, and motivated by desperation, and he came back at me with unexpected vigor. I fell against the shooting bench, knocking the rifle and the sandbag to the floor, and he fell on top of me, his fingers at my throat.

I reached my thumbs up to his eye sockets, but before I could dig out the orbs, Isabelle had the still-hot barrel of the .45 pressed against his temple.

I squirmed out from underneath him and dialed the police. While we waited for them to arrive, I asked Isabelle if she would take a vacation in Utah with me.

"Utah? It's summertime. It'll be incredibly hot," she answered, holding the automatic steadily against Harry Hamilton's head.

"Hot?" I smiled. "You have no idea."

Chapter 41

THE STARSHIP WAS as perfect and responsive as the
day I had bought it. The repairs to the rivetless, composite left wing looked like a long-healed flesh
wound, contributing to my ever-growing perception
of the airplane as an organic being. As Isabelle and I
flew across the Continental Divide, I was filled with
the sense that the airplane was glad to be back under
my command.

I couldn't help thinking about Isabelle's remark to
Hamilton, or Captain Rignola's remarks about my career. I wondered if they were true, and if I was only
kidding myself into thinking that I could regain my
lost sense of self by engaging now and then in a free-
lance investigation.

I glanced behind me to see Isabelle stretched out
on the queen-sized bed, rummaging through a collection of classical compact discs, her bare feet in the
air. Most Starships are set up as working business

aircraft, but mine was laid out more like a flying Winnebago.

"This plane is revoltingly decadent." Her voice wafted forward.

She inserted her selection in the stereo, and the cabin was instantly filled with the strains of Handel's *Wassermusik.*

"That was Uncle Andrew's disc. He loved Handel."

"You can listen to whatever you want now," she said. "He doesn't know or care anymore."

"Yes, he does," I said quietly.

"In that case, he knows that I had to cancel this afternoon's meeting with the AIDS vaccine doctors so that we could go flying off in your million-dollar airplane. Think he'd approve of that? Think that's what he had in mind when he left you the money and told you to do good with it?"

I flicked on the automatic pilot, and was on her in four steps.

"I don't have to justify myself to you," I hissed, grabbing her wrists and shaking her. "My uncle didn't leave me money to put me in bondage, he left it to me because he *loved me!*"

I dropped her wrists and she massaged them.

"That hurt," she said quietly.

"Well, I'm sorry! Sorry that I made mistakes that hurt you. Sorry about Morgan. And Hamilton. I'm sorry you think I've lost my touch."

"I just said that to get Hamilton's attention," she said.

"You could have said a lot of things to get Hamilton's attention. I'm not a saint, all right? I'm the first to admit it. I want to do right by people, but I also want to enjoy my life. Everyone expects things from me, even you. I didn't ask for all this money. I'm doing the best I can. Are you so perfect you can judge me?"

She was quiet for a moment. "It didn't turn out so badly," she said. "You found the counterfeiter, you exposed a fraud."

"And a man died."

I put my hand behind her head and drew her to me. Our noses met, and we smiled as we closed our eyes. I ran my fingers through her blond hair, scratching the top of her head gently with my nails.

"It'll never happen again," I murmured.

She covered my lips with hers.

I pushed her down onto the bed and she lifted her hips for me. Her jeans slid off easily, dry denim on smooth flesh. She wore nothing underneath, and I could feel her and smell her and touch her all at once. She pulled my shirt off violently, ripping the buttons.

She used her mouth on me for a time, but I felt disconnected from her, unwilling to concentrate on my own pleasure, eager to communicate with her on a more equal basis, to set things right. I took her head gently in my hands and brought it up. She looked at me sweetly as she straddled me, her hair framing her face.

The Starship hit a pocket of rough air, making my first thrust harsh. She gasped with pleasure.

"You see?" I said, reaching up for her breasts. "The Starship's your friend after all."

The autopilot pressed on to Moab, and we clung together and shared every molecule of skin, making love over and over, and letting the turbulent sky do half the work.

Chapter 42

ISABELLE WAS GROCERY shopping when Morgan Pajaro came around the side of the house and caught me practicing Wing Chun on the high bluff. There were two newspapers tucked under her arm.

"What a nice surprise," I said.

She threw a copy of the *Los Angeles Times* to the ground.

"Inside cover," she said. Her voice sounded strangled and high. "I'm out on bail."

"Lucky you." I glanced at the article.

"I didn't think you'd be overjoyed."

"You took me," I said matter-of-factly.

"You took me, too."

A hot wind rose up suddenly, blowing the paper away across the red earth. I didn't try to catch it.

She put a hand up to shade her eyes and looked past me at the stringy white clouds on the horizon.

"Everything I've worked for is finished," she said.

"You should have thought of that when you started

counterfeiting," I answered. "You should have left off the little bird."

"That's what Michael said when he found out."

"When he found out," I repeated. "He didn't know?"

She shook her head and smiled.

"All his smooth talk. He was really a simple man."

"You killed him?"

She nodded. "He was going to turn me in. He was going to do what you did."

"How do you know it was me?"

"There's nobody else."

"Harry Hamilton."

"He's a fool. That's why he came to you. He never guessed. Not for years."

"I don't understand. You have such talent, such beauty."

"You wouldn't understand. Men like you never do. Life's a tropical cruise for you. I did it for the money, plain and simple."

She opened her purse and took out a shiny, pearl-handled derringer.

"That's a movie gun," I said.

"It's going to kill you."

"The police will know."

"It doesn't matter anymore."

"Murderers don't get away," I said.

I sat down slowly on the pile of rocks that used to mark the old well. She took a step closer and raised the gun.

"Big talk for a man who's about to die."

"It's about three hundred feet to the bottom." I gestured. The moment I saw her gaze shift to the edge of the bluff, I reached down and shifted the flat rock aside.

"I'm not falling. I'm going to Mexico."

"You won't make it. The desert's too hot. You're sweating already. It looks ugly."

She glanced down at her blouse, and I reached slowly for the rattle-covered tail and jerked the snake out from under the stone. As I rolled to the side, I sent it spinning, body writhing, red mouth wide open and fangs gaping, toward Morgan Pajaro's beautiful face.

Her shot went wild as she threw up her hands to protect herself. The coroner said later that she died so fast because the snake caught her right in the eye with both fangs and two glands full of venom. I told him that I had no idea what Morgan Pajaro was doing down so low.

I guess some people just spend their lives in the dirt.

Arthur Rosenfeld was born in New York in 1957 and attended Yale College, Cornell University, and the University of California. He has worked at a wide variety of jobs, among them: martial arts instructor, corporate officer, and creative director. His interests include photography, motorcycling, scuba diving, exotic tortoise husbandry, sea-kayaking and the challenge of the moment. He lives in Southern California and is the author of numerous magazine articles and books.